GALVESTON CATS

Being the glorious tale
of Great Aunt Meowkin's
Reunion

Davis Many Voices

A LIMITED EDITION
for the 100th Anniversary of
The Great Storm of 1900

Front Cover
(Tabitha and the kitten Pyewackit)
Artist: Robert Hynecek

Back Cover
(Winnie and Meowkin survive the
Great Storm)
Artist: Wes Pitman

ISBN 0-9666438-5-2
Copyright © 2000 by VanJus Press,
1618 -23rd St., Galveston, TX 77550
All Rights Reserved
(409) 762-2333, FAX (409) 762-0411

2

Text Illustrations by Robert Hynecek

Dedication

With much love to my wife Heidi and our sons, Bryan, Ian, and Ethan, who graced these pages with soft paws, for my father, who shared with me a profound love for sea stories, and for my mother and Blossom the cat. And bless the Galveston Cats who inspired me to tell their glorious tales.

If the MoonCat were here now, it would yowl great whiskers.

Contents

Prologue

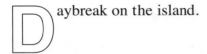aybreak on the island.

The winds offshore rise slightly and the waves slap the empty shoreline with conviction. From the east comes the sun, radiant golden fingers that shiver the darkness and touch the waiting earth with light and warmth. Overhead the screaming gulls screech and prowl the surf for a jack-fish breakfast, and out in the Gulf chug the brave little shrimpers, trawling their nets for the evening's seafood platters. On the great granite boulders that lie in stony heaps near the Seawall the morning light frightens the scavenger crabs lurking in sea-soaked crevices.

And here on one deserted jetty sits a woman in a long dress staring out to sea. A wide-brimmed bonnet crowns her head and every now and then she smiles and weaves a long strand of red hair out of her eyes. Barefoot, she seems to sigh, to rise and fall with the relentless tides that churn and foam and souse her with sea spray.

What thoughts well up in her heart as she sits and contemplates the mystery of the sea? Here on this bit of sandbar of an island naked Indians once feasted on shellfish; pirates caroused on rum and danced on chests of Spanish doubloons; sturdy pioneers raised livestock and merchants exported cotton around the world. And more than once this strip of brown sand has endured howling winds and sheeting squalls. Of all the terrible storms to hit Galveston Island, none was more terrible than the Great Storm of 1900. Terrible was the damage to the city and murderous the loss of human life. And feline.

This is the story of that awesome hurricane and of two plucky survivors who found one another on the beach near where the young woman sits on the tumble of stones and looks out to sea. On the evening of September 8, 1900, Galveston Island lay under water; homes and buildings collapsed under the crushing weight of towering waves, and when the storm passed inland, the city lay in heaps of flattened boards and twisted steel. Perhaps as many as 6,000 human beings—and numberless cats—lost their lives in the Great Storm!

But a young girl named Winnie survived, and on the empty beachhead she found a half-drowned kitten who called herself Meowkin. Together they vowed to dedicate their lives to reinvigorating the shattered community, both human and feline. And when it came time for Meowkin to pass to the Other Shore, she asked the Galveston Cats to break a flounder in her memory and share in the Ceremony at the Seawall.

Unravel now the glorious tale, the true narrative of the Galveston Cats who remember Great-Aunt Meowkin in their hearts and caterwaul before the MoonCat who yowls great whiskers on the occasion of the reunion. Listen as the smiling woman sitting on the jetty with the wind in her hair whispers, "Just visualize, darling."

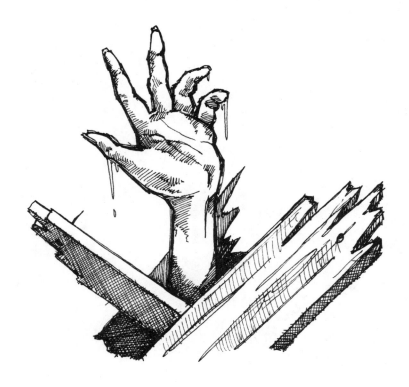

Chapter One:

The MoonCat Yowls Great Whiskers

"Somebody help me, please!"

The faint plea rose from a great pile of debris—planks and boards, fragments of roof, chunks of brick and iron, shards of tin—that lay in heaps on the Gulf side of the island. Pools of sea water freckled the carnage, and everywhere the excess water ran in trickles under the shattered mounds of plywood and timbers and metal.

"Please get me out of here, I'm suffocating!"

The little voice trembled with fear. But there was no one to render aid. The island lay in ruins, flattened as though some unspeakable explosion had flung houses and buildings into the air and scattered the pieces onto the damp, slime-encrusted ground.

Underneath one of the huge piles of planks and boards came the insistent cry.

"I'm dying in here. Please, won't someone help me?"

Blocks away, a family of cats crawled over the

wreckage, stopping every few steps to smooth their wet, tangled fur. Every time the large female cat climbed a drenched mound of crisscrossed planks, she gave out an agonized yowl.

"Meowkin, where are you?"

Her kittens snuggled near the mother cat, still drenched and trembling from their narrow escape. Hidden in the recesses of one of the island's antebellum homes, the cats had waited out the Great Storm, and from behind glass windows had watched the screaming winds tear roofs off buildings, uproot trees, and overturn wagons filled with terror-stricken humans. The cats had screeched as the hurricane like some ferocious boxer had pounded the exposed features of the beautiful city with wave after crushing wave. And at the height of the storm, one of the kittens, Meowkin, had been pulled from the house by the surging waves and disappeared in the tremendous waves.

"Meowkin, please meow for mamma!"

Like frightened ghosts they materialized from their hiding places, the dazed survivors, and stared open-mouthed at the destruction wrought by the sea. Entire blocks of houses lay flattened one atop the other; roofs and foundations lay in snarled heaps everywhere. Here stood a building, intact save for the toothy gaps where thick glass windows once graced a shopkeeper's business; and there, across what had once been a prosperous intersection, a ruined brick shell, its roof collapsed, the once mighty walls tumbled and buried in mud and debris.

Up 18th Street weaved the family of cats, inspecting the waterlogged ruins for any sign of missing Meowkin. The terrified mother cat screeched until her tail frizzed out, and she peeked in shattered buildings oozing sea water and even climbed the top of a shattered telephone pole where she meowed for her lost kitten.

"Meowkin, Meowkin, tell us where you are, please, kitty, kitty, kitty."

But the wind, which had the previous evening howled in excess of one hundred twenty miles an hour, was now a playful sea breeze, and it carried only the stench of death and destruction. Everywhere gobs of evil-smelling slime stained the pitiful remains of the city, as though the Great Storm had with nasty boots walked over the island and crushed into the wet sand houses and buildings and living things.

Fainter and fainter came the mournful meows of the mother cat for her lost kitten. As she and her brood crept under the shadows of flattened homes, the cats saw sights that made their mouths go cotton: naked, mutilated humans hanging weirdly from trees, mangled and bleeding on piles of boards, or smashed beneath piles of rubble.

"I'm NOT going to...die...under these boards," came a defiant voice that rose in intensity as the speaker, buried beneath heaps of soaked lumber steaming in the warm sunlight. Then a scraping sound mingled with a determined groan and the planks and plywood gave way and out crawled—a young girl about ten or eleven.

Picking her way through the mishmash of wood and brick, she emerged into the garish light and blinked reddened eyes. Her swimming dress was torn and shredded and a huge knot bigger than a hen's egg sat above one eye; her hands were bloody and her arms and legs bore deep gashes where the nails had slashed her in the tumultuous waves. Barefoot on the wet ground she stood, surveying the desolate scene.

"Mother! Where are you? Mother!"

In every direction she looked the island seemed utterly destroyed. In the distance stood the unbroken Gresham Mansion and the sad remains of the Sacred Heart Cathedral. Now only the entrance and two spires stood mute witness to the hurricane's fury.

"Why was I saved? Why me? Why did my mother and my brothers and sisters drown and not me?" She cried like her heart would break. Dazed and soaked to the skin, she wandered the ruined streets, sobbing and calling forlornly for her mother, and then, screaming hysterically, begging for her brothers and sisters to answer her.

The only answer was a seagull's raucous screech high overhead and the soft PLOP, PLOP, PLOP of sea water as it slowly dribbled into shallow pools and ebbed away into the gentle breakers massaging the empty beach.

For what seemed hours the weeping child wandered around the forlorn island, sometimes poking into the smothering crush of tumbled houses, sometimes fighting back tears as she called the names of her family. Finally, she came to the beach where the Great Storm had smashed ashore and swamped Galveston Island.

Looking out at the brown waters of the calm Gulf, she screamed, "I hate you! I hate you! You killed my mother and my brothers and sisters." And she kicked her bare feet angrily into the placid waters.

"I wish I were dead! I wish I had the strength to just walk out into the waves and drown. Let the sea finish its work. I hate you!"

She looked around her for something, anything, to throw into the surf and appease her fury, and, to her complete surprise, there, submerged up to her neck in a shallow pool of water, lay a kitten! Tenderly the young girl picked up the still animal and held it close to her heaving chest.

"Poor kitty. The hurricane killed you just like it did my momma and brothers and sisters." She cradled the wet fur tightly and as she squeezed it, water seeped from the kitten's nostrils. Eyes closed, the girl held the kitten under her chin and said a wordless prayer.

Then the kitten suddenly squirmed and meowed loudly in her arms, and the girl raised it above her tangled hair and rejoiced. "Meow, little Meowkin, you're alive!" And indeed the kitten was alive, snorting and spewing water and gasping wetly, but wriggling, writhing, ALIVE!

Chapter Two:

Make Believe with Tabitha and Pyewackit

The old yellow ferryboat gave a mighty toot as motorists began climbing out of their cars to grab a space behind the roped off section of the bow. From this coveted vantage point they stood, braving the wind in their hair and the spray on their faces and laughing at the trickster gulls hovering in mid-air for a tossed bit of bread.

Suddenly a furious honking erupted at the ferryboat's stern and a faded green, very dented Volvo rattled aboard. One of the blue-shirted Coast Guard crew hurried over to the driver's side and tapped on the streaked window. When the window rolled down half-way, the young man spoke.

"Say, lady, this boat's full. You'll have to wait for the next ferry."

A young woman with strawberry red hair dancing across her pretty face leaned her head out the window and pointed at the ferryboat's wake.

"Why can't we take that ferry?," she hollered.

The young man shook his head and long strands of wet brown hair whipped across his cheeks. "Can't lady. The boat's full."

"Oh no, it's not. There's a place right there." And she nodded and pointed to a small opening behind a shiny blue BMW. The blue-shirted crewman looked and stared open-mouthed where the young woman pointed.

"Well, I'll be chowder. You're right, lady. There is a parking space, but I swear there wasn't one there five minutes ago." Lifting his cap, the youthful sailor scratched his head.

"Young man, it's all in how you visualize things." And with that, the smiling red-head gunned her Volvo and screeched the brakes a hiccup away from the sport car's rear bumper. Emerging from the sputtering car, the woman immediately marched to the bow and, nodding at the crowds in front of her, waited as a burly college student stretched and yielded his spot.

Now she had a commanding view of the channel and the anchored steamers down by the east end of the island. As the ferryboat chugged from its moorings, she lifted an enormous purse up to her face and sweetly meowed.

Out of her bag appeared two white ears and then, slowly, the round head of a beautiful white Siamese with eyes as blue as a South Seas lagoon. As it purred, the woman talked softly to the kitten.

"Pyewackit, didn't I tell you we would make it to the ferry on time? And you said if we had one more catnap, we'd never catch the GILCHRIST's afternoon run. Ah, darling, but we did. Are you enjoying the ride? Isn't it delicious feeling the wind and sea rushing around us?"

Pyewackit meowed and leaned farther out of her mistress's purse. Looking across the Bolivar Channel to the landing dock beyond, she said, "Tabitha, this IS magical! I'll bet no cat has ever sailed the Galveston ferryboat and had a front row seat."

Tabitha snuggled the kitten and together they made quiet purring sounds. On either side of them, the passengers were unaware of their presence and continued throughout the ride to talk animatedly among themselves, as though the woman and her cat were not even there.

"I promised to get you to Great-Aunt Meowkin's Reunion, and I'm always as good as my word, Pyewackit. I DO hope you will have a good time. Oh, and Pyewackit. Proper kittens do not associate with garbage cats," Tabitha warned.

The kitten meowed loudly. "I know, Tabitha. You've told me since we got in the car all about party cat manners. Please!" A wavy something floated near the bow and Pyewackit pointed a paw at it.

"What's that, Tabitha?"

"Just a jellyfish. Oh, look! Jars of jellyfishes, Pyewackit." Tabitha raised the purse over her head so that the little Siamese kitten could get a good look at the transparent pods drifting in the current.

"Harmless to cats, but they can certainly sting humans. Down on the public beaches the lifeguards insist on putting meat tenderizer on the welts, as if a jellyfish sting were tenderloin. What they need to do is put tobacco on the burn and that stops the pain but fast." She brought the meowing Pyewackit close to her face and said, ""Look, Pyewackit. Dolphins!"

Sure enough, in the direction Tabitha had pointed, two black fins rolled and dipped, in leisurely pursuit of a shrimpboat trawling up the coast. A huge spiraling of seagulls whirred above the nets, diving and squawking at the harvest of fish.

"Oh, wouldn't it be special to be a seagull," purred Pyewackit. "To be able to fly any time you wanted, to glide over the waves so free. I think that seagulls were pirates in another life, Tabitha."

"Maybe so, darling." Tabitha leaned slightly over the roped area, allowing the sea breeze to stream her long strawberry hair behind her and ripple her long calico peasant dress. From a distance up on the second deck a casual observer might have thought she resembled Merlin's enchantress, the island's version of the Lady of the Lake.

Overhead the seagulls wheeled on a dime, dived like fighter planes into the waves, or chased each like feathered scamps across the blue fabric of the sky. One of the bolder birds landed near the safety boats and stood woodenly like one of the Queen's own Buckingham guards.

"So you want to fly, Pyewackit?" she beamed. "All you have to do is visualize, darling. Watch and do everything I do."

Tabitha carefully placed her bulging purse deckside and Pyewackit plopped herself on the zippers for a closer look. Taking four measured breaths, Tabitha closed her eyes and then very slowly raised her arms above her head, as though in prayer. She slowly threw back her head and stood, trance-like, as the sea spray dashed across the bow, soaking her bare feet.

If Tabitha can visualize becoming a seagull, thought the kitten, so can I. Closing her blue eyes, Pyewackit inhaled deeply through her wet nose and held out her wet paws. Visualize, she told herself.

Out of the blackness that was a dream hovered, mistlike, a pair of wings, white with black tips, bent like flaps on an old Navy training plane. Pyewackit opened her emerald eyes and saw she was soaring in the clouds.

"Am I flying?" The rush of wind was incredible and all around her was the emptiness of air. "I AM flying!"

Suddenly another pair of white wings came into view and a clear, high voice shouted to the amazed kitten. "You ARE flying, Pyewackit. We are both flying." And Pyewackit, looking up, saw the shining face of Tabitha, her flashing eyes sparkling like fire opals, smiling down at her.

They wheeled and they rolled; they played tail tag

and run and shoot; they plummeted head-first into the salty waves, wriggling like eels underwater; finally, soaring into the light with dripping feathers and grasping tiny fish in their hooked beaks.

Then they found the air pocket where the cool winds ruffle the tail feathers and Tabitha and Pyewackit glided effortlessly across the island. Coming out of a wide turn, they gathered speed and climbed high above the ferryboat's wave-shattering bow. There, where the air rushed in cold breaths, the two seagulls locked wings and screamed loudly. Then, as though pirouetting on empty air, they dropped like white stones just in front of the chugging ferryboat.

Tabitha retrieved her bonnet under the driver's seat and tucked a stray strand of red hair behind her ear while Pyewackit licked her white paws and freshened her whiskers. Leaning far over the bow, Tabitha whispered, "Wasn't that just TOO GLORIOUS for words, darling?"

Pyewackit purred and purred. "I've never done anything like that before, Tabitha. How did you learn such a trick?"

The pretty woman with diamonds in her eyes smiled and said, "Just something my grandmother Winnie taught me one day when I lay in bed with a cold. 'Visualize, Tabitha,' she told me. 'Focus with intent on your dreams, and one day you shall soar.' And you know what, darling? Grandmother Winnie was right."

Pyewackit licked the white fingers of her mistress, and in turn, she received several gentle pats. "You know what, Tabitha? You are the best human pet any cat could ever have."

A single tear sprang from one corner of Tabitha's eye, and she reached down and hugged the kitten. "Oh, Pyewackit."

Just then the young Coast Guardsman who had stopped Tabitha on the Bolivar side of the channel shouted behind them. "Time to get back in your cars, ladies and gentlemen. We should be landing in another two minutes."

As Tabitha turned to retrace her steps to the ancient Volvo, the attendant stared at her. "It's you again. How did you get a spot near the bow if you parked your car down at the stern?"

Smiling like the Cheshire cat, Tabitha sniffed, "I told you young man, visualization is everything." Once safely in her car, skirts folded neatly beneath her, she waved at the crewman and when he came up to the window, Tabitha observed, "And another thing, young man. When is this old tug going to have refreshments served on board? My kitten and I have a craving sometimes for fresh cream. And in a saucer, of course."

Then the GILCHRIST docked on Galveston Island and, revving up the ancient engine, Tabitha meshed the gears over the metal railing as Pyewackit waved a white paw through the rear window at the astonished youth.

Chapter Three:

The Strand Under Water

Down Market Street rattled the old Volvo, and Pyewackit wondered where Tabitha was going. Peeking out of her mistress' purse, she asked if they were headed for The Strand, once the old warehouse district on the island, and now refurbished into a tourist mecca of t-shirt shops and fajita restaurants, antique hideaways and po-boy bistros.

"We have a little time before Great-Aunt Meowkin's Reunion," answered Tabitha, "and I thought you might enjoy sharing a shrimp salad with me. And besides," she smiled, "there's something I want you to visualize with me."

Pyewackit sulked in the purse, and while she licked a paw and brushed the white hair out of her eyes, she grumbled under her breath. "I don't want to sit out on some dumb table and watch pale humans in bunny shirts wander in and out of these old warehouses. And I'm not really hungry for shrimp salad. But oh no, we have to do what Tabitha wants to do."

Sometimes Pyewackit could behave very aristocatic.

Unbelievably, Tabitha cruised into The Strand and

immediately found a parking spot near the Old Strand Emporium. Up the steps they went, and Pyewackit, despite herself, perked up at the overwhelming odors of sizzling fajitas and grilled tuna. "I'm going cat-atonic from hunger," she growled.

Finding a table in front of a little storefront sandwich parlor, Tabitha ordered a large shrimp salad and two glasses of half-and-half. The girl behind the counter claimed not to have any of the rich cream, but Tabitha only nodded at the cooler behind the register, and when the refrigerator door was opened, there sat an old-fashioned milk jug of half-and-half. Paying for the meal, Tabitha smirked and said, "Young woman, you should visualize more often."

Munching little kitty bites out of the delicious salad, Tabitha and Pyewackit enjoyed the late afternoon pedestrian traffic. On the sidewalk lurched four hulking boys wearing red bandanas looped over their long, straggly hair. They look like LaFitte's pirates, Pyewackit shuddered. Here came a middle-aged couple, obviously Midwesterners, who had never seen this many shell shops in their lives. She wore a very tight-fitting pair of cranberry shorts and matching top, while he paraded about in yellow canary shorts and a Tom and Jerry cartoon t-shirt.

Tabitha and Pyewackit sniggled like kittens on a catnip ride at the outrageously dressed tourists. A gaggle of young girls emerged from a general store, their mouths swollen with peppermint sticks. Tabitha whispered to Pyewackit, who frowned at the girls' screaming laughter,

"Those girlies have some mighty short shorts on, don't they, darling?" The kitten nodded and wondered why some female humans wore such skimpy outfits. Did it have anything to do with being stopped by pirate boys and yelled at all the time, she asked herself.

During a lull in the tourist traffic, Pyewackit laid a paw on Tabitha's freckled arm and said, "I'm full, Tabitha. Don't you think we ought to be going now. We don't want to be late for Great-Aunt Meowkin's Reunion, do we?"

Tabitha yawned and stretched herself like a pampered housecat and smacked her red lips. "Now, speaking of Great-Aunt Meowkin, darling, did you know that she and my grandmother Winnie lived through the Great Storm of 1900? In a way, they were unique, Winnie and Meowkin. Both were the youngest females in their litters, and they met the morning after the storm."

Pyewackit shook her furry head. "No, I never heard that story at all. And I'll bet I'm the only kitten on the island who was invited to Great-Aunt Meowkin's Reunion. Did you have anything to do with that, Tabitha?"

But Tabitha only put one long finger to her lips and shook her head. Looking out across the street where trollies once rattled on iron rails, Tabitha continued her story. "Yes, Great-Aunt Meowkin and Grandmother Winnie survived the worst natural disaster in this country's history. The hurricane blew in about two hours before dawn on Saturday morning, September 8. By midmorning this entire area," and she waved her hands from The Strand and gestured beyond the historical landmark on Seawall Boulevard where Fort Crockett once stood at the water's edge, "was under 15 feet of water, darling."

Pyewackit tried to imagine everything in her range of vision—the shops, the tourists, the cars—submerged or floating, but the thought overwhelmed. "I just can't imagine, Tabitha."

The red-haired woman undid her bonnet and shook free her long, beautiful red hair. "Then let's visualize, darling, and you'll see what I mean." Kitten and human closed their eyes and then Tabitha nodded.

Out of the darkness Pyewackit heard a terrible roaring in her ears, like a freight train running through her head. Then she felt the wind and spray on her face and heard the waves from the Gulf as they lapped over her paws. Across the street a five foot swell crashed into the brick warehouse and the roof collapsed. The wind howled and windows shattered in all the buildings. Debris from the buildings or homes rushed down the street in a swirling, foaming tide of watery death.

A doghouse floated by with a small terrier chained to it. The poor dog barked pitifully as it sailed past. Great beams of wood and plankings dipped and rolled in the rising flood, and here and there, through the torrent of rain and wind and thundering water, a victim—a wailing child, an hysterical woman or cursing man—fought the waves and bobbed about like a spinning cork.

Then a two-wheeled carriage floated past, the horse struggling with the reins, and a man in a soaked business suit trying desperately to untie the strap wrapped around his waist. Suddenly, carriage, horse and driver slipped beneath the deadly waters and disappeared. The wind whipped savagely down the swirling, debris-filled street, now running nearly nine feet deep in churning brown waters that slammed against the brick warehouses with the harsh blows of the seven angry gods of the sea. In twenty-four hours the Great Storm had ravaged the island with two thousand million tons of rain.

Then the winds blew themselves out and the rising waves began to recede. Telephone poles and cables lay twisted like spaghetti in the muddy streets thick with splintered boards and the dead, swollen bodies of animals and people. Only the skeletal remains of the stately City Hall remained. Roofs sagged; sidewalks reeked of heaps of slime; grass shards rose like evil thorns in the carnage of boards, sliding, and metal. In some places the destruction stood two stories high.

Dazed, numbed, grey with fear and disbelief, the survivors in twos and threes crept from their shelters and surveyed the damage. The sea had battered the island city, bloodied and pummeled the people and their homes, swallowed like some monstrous leviathan this Jonah of a sandbar and sent it swirling, roaring, spewing into the maw of the beast and then spat it out in muddy pools.

Pyewackit felt something wet and cold running down her head and her white fur went electric. "Help me,

Tabitha, I'm drowning. Save me!" But then the something wet and cold tasted, indeed, WAS half-and-half. The little Siamese looked up to see Tabitha grinning down at her and shaking the last few drops of the cream on her kitten face.

"That wasn't nice at all," fumed Pyewackit. "And I wasn't scared!"

Tabitha chortled. "Of course you weren't, darling. Sometimes, though, what you visualize CAN be a little frightening. Well, are we ready to go? Musn't keep our friends waiting. Tonight is Great-Aunt Meowkin's Reunion."

Pyewackit batted her baby blues and inquired, "Who will be at the reunion tonight, Tabitha?"

Sighing softly to herself, the pretty red-haired young woman responded, "I just wonder...."

Chapter Four:

One-Eyed Tom Pipes the News

"Avast there, ye overstuffed excuses for a throw rug, stand at attention. I got important news to pipe." One-Eyed Tom, the crab cat, shifted his chew and glared down at the two plump Manx tomcats sunning themselves on the huge granite boulders behind the Galveston Seawall.

Rumpy yawned at the fierce-looking cat with the right eye shut tight like an unsmiling mouth. He licked a front paw and continued combing his whiskers while Stumpy, who loved to tease the old tomcat, growled his displeasure.

"What brings a mudcrab cat down to the Seawall to see us?" asked Stumpy, his nub of a tail twitching nervously. "Why aren't you out in the tides digging for crabs?"

Rumpy joined in. "Yah. Getting your paws stinking wet and your nose pinched by stupid crabs. Why don't you prowl the beaches for mullet? These shores are littered with washed-up breakfast."

"Belay that talk, matey," hissed One-Eyed Tom. "I be here on official business, or I wouldn't waste me time on fleabait like youse."

Stumpy and Rumpy hissed in unison, but the old tomcat continued his tirade.

"Today be the 8th of September. Do ye know the terrible significance of this day, lads?" One-Eyed Tom looked back and forth at the two tubby tabbies with his one good yellow eye.

The brothers stared at each other and shrugged striped shoulders. "Nah," said Stumpy. "You tell us."

"Sea spawn! Sons of sea worms! Tonight is the anniversary of the passing of Great-Aunt Meowkin and all the Galveston Cats will be caterwaulin' the night away in her honor. 'Course, if you two bloated pussycats maybe got something better to do, like kiss a jellyfish's behind, don't bother to come." One-Eyed Tom made as though to go, but Rumpy grabbed the old crabber's bushy tail.

"Why should we sophisti-cats bother with Great-Aunt Meowkin's Reunion? What makes her so special?" Rumpy sniffed, a mouthful of hair between clenched teeth.

"Yah barnacle brains," exclaimed One-Eyed Tom. "Great-Aunt Meowkin treated me wounded eye when a monstrous swordfish plucked it out of me socket off the coast of Java. Soothed the pain with her healing herbs, she did, and got me back on me feet in two shakes of a Manta Ray. Anything else yah hairballs want to know 'bout why I'm makin' cat tracks for the reunion tonight?" One-Eyed Tom squinted at the lounging felines.

"No lie, One-Eyed Tom?" Stumpy asked incredulously. Tonight really is the reunion? All the Galveston Cats—even the kitties from The Strand—will be there?" Stumpy tugged the old crabber's bushy tail.

"Leggo my tail, shrimp bait!" howled One-Eyed Tom. Doncha wish YOUSE GUYS had a tail to holt onto, ye yeller varmints." One-Eyed Tom again tried to leave, but Stumpy held on tight.

"Great leaping sailfish, brother," yowled Stumpy. "Think of the kitties that will be there."

"And the flounder!" shouted Rumpy.

"The Strand is Reputation City for the finest kitties to stretch their tails between here and South Padre," Stumpy whooped.

"Leggo my tail, ye frog's behind, afore I scratch out yer eyes!" One-Eyed Tom spat at the brothers.

"And the halibut!" Rumpy rejoiced, licking his lips.

"You tell the rest of the Galveston Cats that Stumpy and Rumpy will be there with white paws on," screeched Stumpy.

One-Eyed Tom yanked his tail from Stumpy's grasp and stared hard at the plump cats. "Ah, I hope the sand crabs eats yer innards." Then he leaped from the boulders to the Seawall, raised his tail, and gave both brothers a good squirt of the old tom.

"Now ye's marked with One-Eyed Tom's scent," hissed the old crabber. "Youse sea slugs'll need a hot bath now afore ye go callin' on respectable cats." Laughing like a disturbed seagull, One-Eyed Tom pranced down Seawall Boulevard, his tail twitching crazily in the morning breeze.

"Ugh, ugh, ugh!" The twin Manx screamed like kites tearing at a beached grouper, dived into the surf, and then rolled vigorously in the wet sand.

"I'll get that stupid one-eyed cat," sputtered Rumpy. "He can't spray us and prance away like that."

"Oh, blow it out your ear, Rumpy," growled Stumpy, energetically licking his paw and washing out his ears.

"Yeah, right," retorted his brother. "Do you have any idea how hard it is to wash your back when there's no tail to balance on? Uh, maybe you do. Ohhh, I hate that one-eyed excuse for a cologne factory."

"Just help me smooth down this midriff pooch, and then I'll do yours, Rumpy," insisted Stumpy. "Hey, where's that fish spine comb I loaned you last week?"

"Your fish spine comb? HA! That was my fish spine comb. I found it on the beach last week and loaned it to you," howled Rumpy.

"Did not!"

"Did too!"

38

"Did NOT!"

"Did TOO!"

Suddenly a huge bucket of blood bait sailed over the Seawall and drenched both cats, who came up sputtering and spitting.

"Now ye can have the rest o' the day with One-Eyed Tom's permission to clean up afore ye get shore leave." And with those taunting words, One-Eyed Tom sauntered down the sidewalk like he owned it. An early morning tourist wearing a green parrot shirt and camouflage shorts wobbled by on a shaking bicycle and, dodging the veteran of the shrimp wars, flew headfirst over the handlebars and landed bottoms-up on the curb.

"Drop anchor," grinned the crabber. "Me ship's got the right of way in this here channel." And leaping a stuffed trash can heaped with styrofoam cups and greasy paper plates, he pranced down the empty beach. In his wake One-Eyed Tom left behind two yowling cats combing fish chunks out of their eyes and one very angry tourist who waved a fist in the air and sputtered like a backfiring go-cart.

"We'll never get to Great-Aunt Meowkin's Reunion at this rate," moaned Rumpy to Stumpy, pounding his brother with one crimson-slick paw.

Chapter Five:

Sailing with the Pirates

Across the street two half-naked boys skating rollerblades swirled to a stop, howled gales of laughter at the overturned tourist and made barking sounds deep in their throats.

Bright red bandanas hooked over their long, stringy hair, the blade runners started up the street, laughing like pirates with "X" marks the spot in their evil eyes. Up ahead the sidewalk rose invitingly—a daredevil place for screaming blades. On impulse the boys dashed for the concrete swell.

Suddenly two interlocked furry tails like unfurled sails came into view and then a large, grey Korat materialized, escorting a small Persian blue tabby. Too late! By the time the two cats saw what hit them, the boys were halfway down the street, cawing like gangsta crows.

The grey cat leaped to his feet and immediately threw his front paws into his best Ninja stance. "BAN-ZAI!" he yowled.

"Come back, you gulls' heinies, and feel paws of steel." He hopped madly from padded paw to bared claw. "Blindside me and not show colors, you jackfish. Come back here and feel dragon punch." The Korat raked the air with angry claws and his white headband tattooed with the rising sun snapped angrily in the breeze. Then he saw the Persian tabby on her side and rushed to her.

"Miss Panders, oh so sorry. Please to get up. Did those jack nastyfaces hurt you? Please to stand now!"

The Persian blue tabby slowly fluttered her amber eyes, looked into the silver whiskers and green eyes of her worried friend. "Oh, Jules, why do humans have to be so mean?"

She bounded up and began giving herself a bath. As she brushed her flanks, the Korat licked her lavender shoulders.

"If those shagnasties come back, I shred them with hungry dragon claws." And Ninja Jules hissed and spat a nearby dandelion dead to the ground.

"Oh, Jules, where EVER did you learn such an exotic language? Is it true what the Galveston Cats say, that you went to sea before you were weaned?" Miss Panders looked up with worshipful eyes at Ninja Jules, who was still practicing double kick and punch moves.

"That right, sweet lady. Before I three weeks old, I whip my weight in nurse sharks. I sailed with hard captains who gave me octopus milk in coconut shells for breakfast. I rode electric eels in the South Pacific and walked from here to Matamores on necks of horseshoe crabs. I am great-great-great-great-great grandson of Admiral Kawaguchi Sushi, the cat who sailed with fierce pirate captain LaFitte."

Miss Panders patted the pouf between her glistening pointed ears and gave a little kitty-like sneeze. When her glorious long-haired tail rose like a captain's flag midships, she took Ninja Jules by the paw and pulled him along.

"We can't be late for Great-Aunt Meowkin's Reunion, Jules. Let's hurry, and while we go, tell me about that terrible pirate LaFitte." Miss Panders purred as Ninja Jules squeezed her paw with his own thick pads.

"You haven't heard story how Admiral Kawaguchi single-pawedly save pirate captain's neck? I tell story now, Miss Panders."

"Eight days out of New Orleans pirates spy fat Spanish galleon and two small escorts. 'Loaded with gold and jewels,' shouted LaFitte, the pirate captain, 'all hands on deck. I plan to board her and take my plunder.'

"Our sixteen guns shattered the stillness and filled air with thick, billowy smoke. The two escorts turned bows and whimpered all the way back to Spain. LaFitte brought ship alongside floating treasure chest and demanded Spanish dog strike white flag. Not even LaFitte expected dog of a Madrid captain to return fire, but he did, raking sides with chains and nails.

"Half a dozen pirates pitched into foaming deeps right then and there, and LaFitte ordered remaining men to swing aboard, and they did. Then it was hand-to-hand fighting, and pirates made chowder of Spanish whelps.

LaFitte was everywhere, stabbing, slashing, cursing at pirates to throw cowardly Spanish dogs to sharks.

"Then Kawaguchi saw huge sailor leap from captain's bridge smack onto LaFitte and knock him to deck where both men struggled with loaded pistol. Kawaguchi leaped from rope to rope until directly below laughing enemy who now standing over body of unconscious captain. Just as he leveled pistol at LaFitte's head, brave Kawaguchi dived like sea hawk, claws outstretched, straight at enemy's neck. He made direct hit, tearing at Spanish dog's cheeks and eyes. In less than a heartbeat, captain leaped from the burning deck and run howling enemy through with razor-sharp cutlass. Then and there, brave LaFitte gave Kawaguchi battlefield promotion. He became Admiral Kawaguchi, the Grey Avenger."

Ninja Jules paused and licked his paws and stroked his whiskers. "And that who escorting you to reunion tonight, Miss Kitty Kakes." He accepted the deep, throaty purring from Miss Panders, who cuddled the sleek gray shoulder. Their tails interlocked and writhed like snakes. The romantic moment, however, was spoiled by a tremendous screaming hurtling at them on black rollerblades.

"It's those meanies on their rollerblades," yelled Miss Panders. "Do something, Jules, before they run over us again."

The two boys aimed directly for the cats, when to their utter surprise, the powerful Korat inflated himself and, screaming "BANZAI!" rushed at them like a runaway buzz saw. The last thing the two blade runners saw was a whirring fuzzy cloud of teeth and claws that scratched and hissed and bit, a gray dervish of feline ferociousness, that's what Miss Panders thought as the two boys rolled slowly away, rubbing bloody wounds and sobbing loudly.

"You really ARE related to a pirate captain," gushed Miss Panders. "You're my treasure," purred the tail-switching lavender tabby.

Ninja Jules looked into the adoring eyes of Miss Panders and his heart leaped like a sailfish. How I get lucky, he asked himself. Then he locked his slender gray tail on her bushy blue one and they strolled down the street together.

"So tell me, Miss Panders, did great Aunt-Meowkin know any pirates?"

Miss Panders squeezed Jules' tail tighter and nodded. "She knew just about everything that happened on this island, Jules. I don't think she was alive when your great-whatever grandfather sailed with LaFitte and his pirates, but she used to tell us kittens the story about the time when the Pirates and the Indians had a doubleheader."

Miss Panders watched Ninja Jules shake his head and stare blankly at her. Then she nipped his ears and grinned. "That's how Great-Aunt Meowkin used to teach us kittens to listen to her story."

Ninja Jules looked puzzled. "But double-headers...I'm afraid you have to explain baseball story, Miss Panders."

"I promise, Jules. We have just enough time and enough blocks left to tell the story before we arrive at the reunion. Will Percey and Evelyn be there, do you think?"

"Oh, those two bachelor Chartreux, who knows? I thought they would have retired to abbey in France by now. Maybe they retire and live like pampered cats in Casa del Mar balcony suite."

Miss Panders licked Jules' gray ear and his back arched in the air. "Oh, hush now and listen to my story," meowed Miss Panders, snuggling against her kung-fu feline cat-friend. "I can't think of another story that would please Great-Aunt Meowkin on her reunion night."

48

Chapter Six:

The Pirates and Indians Doubleheader

hile Miss Panders paused to fluff her whiskers and give her glorious tail a quick paw-over, a divebombing gull slammed into the brown waters of the Gulf, snagged a mullet in its strong beak, and careening on one white and black wing, wheeled ninety degrees above the waves and landed on the weatherbeaten railing of the old Balinese Room, the island's notorious nightclub from years past.

Ninja Jules watched the hungry scavenger bird quickly fillet the writhing thing on the casino's splintered railing and swallow beakfuls of fish flesh. The boarded-up, dilapidated nightclub, which for decades had tempted tourists with rhumba bands and big band entertainers, now stretched forlornly into the Gulf, a haven for the restless gulls.

"Please to hear, Miss Panders, if you know secrets of Balinese Room?" asked Ninja Jules.

Miss Panders, between kitty licks and nibbles at her glorious tail, shook her little head and continued her paw-over. For cats, even abandoned trash bag rippers, spend an extraordinary amount of their time giving themselves a paw-over, which is like a trip to the beauty parlor and the cosmetics counter all tongued into one.

As Miss Panders finished her rinse and licked herself dry, Ninja Jules recalled what he had heard from Trips' great-uncle Aloysius, who had once worked as a rodent bouncer on the fabled nightclub's deck. Great-uncle Aloysius had never fully explained what went on out on the T-head end of the Balinese pier, but in his catnip cups, he spun exotic tales of what he had seen and heard.

You had to walk past the bar and cross the dining room where the music was very Latin and very loud, great-uncle Aloysius confided, and down a long hallway and past the kitchen. Ninja Jules remembered that Trips' aging relative laughed when he told how his human pet, a Chinese cook named Shanghai Jimmy, used to fish for sea trout through a trap door behind the cauldrons of steaming food. If guests were escorted through a series of six heavy glass doors, then they had arrived, great-uncle Aloysius whispered, his matted black eyebrows rising like ominous clouds over the yellow islands of his eyes, in the kingdom of one-armed bandits.

Try as he might, Ninja Jules could never get Trips' great-uncle to say exactly what the kingdom of the one-armed bandits WAS, or for that matter, why a respectable nightclub like the Balinese Room would bother to hire one-armed thieves to pester the guests. Great-uncle Aloysius would only give Ninja Jules a Cheshire cat grin and tell Ninja Jules that when it came to late-night wheeling and dealing in the back rooms, he was better off uninformed. When Ninja Jules became a full-grown cat, the Balinese Room had closed forever and great-uncle Aloysius had retired to Brunswick, Maine, where he ran an antique shop with a little tea room off to one side where he displayed his rodent trophies.

"So you don't know any more secrets than that?" asked Miss Panders, fluffing her whiskers into aristo-cat perfection.

"Have no idea what happen to Shanghai Jimmy," responded Ninja Jules. "Maybe he fall through trapdoor one night and roll out to sea in high tide. Shanghai Jimmy may wash ashore on China mainland some day," grinned the fighting Korat, his martial arts headband flying its colors defiantly in the morning breeze.

"That just leaves the Flagship then," singsonged Miss Panders, pointing a paw at the huge hotel rising like an Ice Capades castle over the Gulf. "And I don't know any Galveston Cats that have worked there as rodent bouncers."

"Please to inquire at reunion tonight," yawned Ninja Jules. "Now what about Pirates and Indians doubleheader story, Miss Panders?"

Waving her glorious tail in the air, Miss Panders meowed like a kitten hungry for cream. "Sure thing, you karate cat!"

Ninja Jules rubbed shoulders with Miss Panders and their glorious tails intertwined. For some moments the two cats purred their hearts out, oblivious to the screech of tires and squeal of brakes. On Seawall Boulevard, the traffic — motorist and pedestrian alike — moved as restlessly as the tides held back by the huge concrete walls that long ago Great-Aunt Meowkin had urged the Galveston Cats to raise and hurl back the raging storms in the Gulf.

In mid-purr the two cats' loving embrace was interrupted by an angry motorist who narrowly avoided colliding with a brown van full of kids attempting to ease into the flow of traffic. Gruffly the BOI—a bona-fide "born on island" native—behind the wheel demanded to know if the tourist was a recent graduate of some croaker-headed driving school. Both motorists shook their fists in the air as pedestrians swelled the sidewalks and cars in tight formation waited for the light to change.

"Cat-fucius say, 'Motorist like tropical storm—all wind and growl, but blow over quick.' Please to tell story now, Miss Panders," begged Ninja Jules, nodding his gray head vigorously.

"Now Great-Aunt Meowkin heard this from a Somali cat whose family ate out of the oyster cairns left by the Indians who once lived on this island. The Indian men were very, very tall and they wore bamboo canes through their noses. And in all weather the Karankawa, for that's what they called themselves, stalked the beaches, carrying their long bows and fishing the shallow inlets.

"The Karankawa rubbed shark oil on their bodies and not even the mosquitos would bite them. And they used nets to catch delicious fish and clams which they sometimes fed to prowling cats and everybody ate just like family.

"One day some mean pirates came spying on the Indian camp. They laughed to themselves, thinking they would possess new wives that very night. While the Indian women were collecting sea peas along the beach, the pirates sneaked up and grabbed them! And they carried the screaming squaws back to LaFitte's fort.

"When the Karankawa discovered that two of their women had been kidnapped, they held a conference and decided to attack the pirate camp. They rolled in the dirt, jumped over the fire, and painted themselves with red clay. Then they seized their long bows and arrows and went whooping and shouting into the underbrush after the pirates.

"Back at the pirate camp, your great-whatever's human pet, the pirate LaFitte, was holding a meeting with his men. Should they fight the Karankawa or return the Indian women to their tribe?

"While the pirates were arguing, the air suddenly became alive with arrows. Pointed barbs of fish spine whizzed through the air, striking the walls of the fort, the shutters, the wagons, and the horses. One or two of the pirates looked like inflated blowfish.

"LaFitte knew his only chance to survive the Indian attack was to fire his cannons at the bloodthirsty warriors, and he called for the two pirates who had stolen the women to climb the ramparts and fire the cannon at the Karankawa who were running circles around the fort and whooping fit to bust."

Ninja Jules stopped walking and licked his flank. "And two pirates stupid enough to dodge arrows and fire cannons at angry Indians?"

Miss Panders nodded. "It was either the Indians' arrows or LaFitte's cutlass. They looked like pincushions by the time they got the cannons loaded, but somehow they managed to fire a round at their screaming attackers and the noise and smoke and roar scattered the Karankawa like sand crabs."

The slim blue Korat scratched his left ear. "But you said Great-Aunt Meowkin teased you about doubleheader. Where baseball?"

Miss Panders made smacking sounds like she was eating softboiled eggs. "Just listen, silly. To keep the peace with the Karankawa, Lafitte had to return the two squaws, which Great-Aunt Meowkin said was only fair, and the two mean pirates. Well, they were full of holes anyway, so LaFitte turned their bodies over to the Indians, who scalped them both."

Ninja Jules glared at Miss Panders. "So! Where doubleheader?"

Miss Panders waved her bushy tail across Ninja Jules' astonished eyes. "So yourself! The Karankawa now had two peeled pirate heads—a doubleheader if I ever heard of one—whenever they went fishing or hunting. The Karankawa believed the pirate heads brought them good luck. Do you think humans believe that way now, Jules?"

Licking his paws and waving his spit curls backwards, Ninja Jules shrugged his powerful shoulders. "It hard to tell what humans believe, Miss Panders. I mean, these two-leggeds take OFF clothes to wade in water and they howl about burning suntan. Please to know if happy that we cats, Miss Panders. We take our fur coats with us wherever we go, and we never get tan."

Miss Panders smiled. "You're not only brave, Jules, you're smart. Curiosity may have got some cats, but Jules, the SMARTS got you. Oh, but hurry! We'll be late for Great-Aunt Meowkin's Reunion."

And the two cats quickened their pace, tails winding and unwinding in the air. Somewhere out in the Gulf two black fins sliced through the waters and a tall, thin, yellow-striped cat leaning against a stucco wall heaved a deep sigh.

Chapter Seven:

Seven Fathoms Deep with a Tiger Shark

By late morning the island pulsates with human activity, and the first waves of tourists have made the rounds of shops at The Strand, hiked the soft beach in search of unbroken hermit crab shells, or hustled the kids out to Seawall Park for a picnic outing and a tour of the WW II ships anchored at the pier where Great-Aunt Meowkin once fished for flounder.

As the two lovestruck cats frisked past the grand dame of all the island's seafaring inns, the Hotel Galvez, a long, lean yellow-striped cat stared blankly at the performing dolphins. Then, as if on signal, he licked a paw and stroked his stump of a left hind leg. For several moments he gazed out at the Gulf, and at last he released his hold and growled half-heartedly.

"Twelve year it been since me leg got bit off by a tiger shark, and here the stump goes to hurtin' at the mere sight of dogfish. Belay there, leg. It won't do no good to throb fer the rest of yah, the shark chewed it off and the shark rests at the bottom of Davy Jones' locker."

He interrupted his grumblings to glare at Ninja Jules and Miss Panders mincing across the street. The slim Korat saw the old Havana Brown cat propped up against the hotel wall and waved to him.

"Come on now, Chester, stir stump, will you? It getting on time for Great-Aunt Meowkin's Reunion." Ninja Jules arched his back, Halloween-style. "Going to be whole beach of kitties from Strand, we hear. MEOW!"

Miss Panders pretended to frizz her glorious tail, and then she waved at Chester. "Please join us."

Chester nibbled some weeds near the double door entrance. "Got too many other important things to do than gossip with a bunch of society cats."

At the intersection, Ninja Jules and Miss Panders plaited their tails. "Last chance, Chester," hollered Ninja Jules.

Chester nibbled the grass angrily and refused to look up.

Before she disappeared from view, Miss Panders yowled, "They'll be serving flounder tonight, Chester."

Chester took a deep swallow of the awful-tasting saliva grass ball and spit it half-way across the hotel's manicured front lawn. "Wait up, shipmates, I'm a-comin'." And with that the tawny, scrawny cat padded and stumped, stumped and padded his way through the mad tourist traffic and lurched to a stop at the curb and stared at the twosome.

"Have I ever told you cats how I lost me leg?" Chester intoned. He walked, for all his gimpiness, like THE only tomcat with a mission on the entire island.

Ninja Jules grimaced. "At least thousand times. And every time I hear story, it change. One time, it shark get your leg, another time it killer whale, and next time...."

Miss Panders shushed Ninja Jules with her bushy lavender tail. "Why, Chester, seems like I've never heard you tell that story. Why don't you share it with us while we go to Great-Aunt Meowkin's Reunion?"

"Be happy to, Miss Panders," smirked Chester. Ninja Jules took an air of pretended snobbishness which isn't very hard for cats to do, and Chester cleared his throat, lit his well-used corncob pipe, and began amusing the cat couple with an old sea adventure he called "Seven Fathoms with a Tiger Shark."

"Now listen, you cats, every word I'm about to tell you is true as John Paul Jones' swashbuckles..."

Ninja Jules hissed like a cobra and his tail danced angrily in the air. Miss Panders made a face and nodded to Chester, who had finally fired his pipe.

"Me and Cap'n Peleg, me human pet, had worked coastal waters for eight days without enough haul to feed Jules here. One mornin' captain looks me in the eyes and says, 'Chester, they ain't no shrimp in these waters. Let's put some distance 'tween us and land.' And we did. For four days and nights we sailed 'till there weren't nothin' but blue sky above us and blue water beneath us."

Chester puffed extravagantly, blowing little arching dolphins in the air. Then he continued.

"We let down the nets and plowed that piece of ocean for the shrimp harvest we could take. Believe me, we just HAULED it in. In about five hours we had filled every ice chest and bucket with big, fat shrimp. Then Cap'n Peleg, he did a real stupid thing."

Ninja Jules purred. "He decide NOT use you for bait, right, Chester?"

Chester glared at Ninja Jules and stopped to stroke his throbbing stump. "Durn sea snake. Kitty, if you only knew how this gnawed-up leg hurts to walk on, you wouldn't be so smarty-cat."

"Oh, go on, Chester. I'm just thrilled to hear your story." Miss Panders stuck her tongue out at Ninja Jules, who wearily shook his head. But when he tried to unwind his tail from Miss Panders' tail, she smiled at the Thai cat like she could grin canary feathers.

"Did you know Great-Aunt Meowkin?" asked Miss Panders.

"Know her!" Chester coughed and black smoke erupted from the old Havana Brown's ears. "Know Great-Aunt Meowkin, Miss Panders? I owe me life to that dear feline. See, after me shark attack, Great-Aunt Meowkin, she bandaged me leg with healing salves and inside a week she had me a new leg to stump around on. Dang me for a sea cucumber if I wouldn't be the cat's meow if I was wearin' it now. But nobody tole me formal attire was necessary." Chester paused, scratched his short brown hair, and nodded.

"Great-Aunt Meowkin, she pretty much saved me from the Deep Six, she did."

Miss Panders placed a soft paw on Chester's shoulder and let out a soft sigh.

"Thanks, Miss Panders. Now, where was I? Oh yes. Cap'n Peleg, he ups and cleans all the trash fish over the side—croakers and puffers, mainly—when off to port bow this huge black fin slices through the water. I sees it and goes to clawin' me human pet's leg, but he don't see that ugly fin sawin' the water, and he kicks me all the way to the stern. Then, just as he's about to pitch a bucket of fish heads overboard, blast me for an electric eel if that bully shark don't leap entirely out of the water and land on deck!"

Chester took a deep pull on his pipe for effect and cut his eyes around at Miss Panders, who was standing on the edge of her paws, and then back to Ninja Jules, whose gray hair was standing on end. Then he continued.

"Well, that tiger shark was twenty feet long if he was a guppy, and he started crunchin' everything in his way—buckets, netting, rope—and he was a-chompin' straight for Cap'n. I knew it was up to me to save me captain, so's I leaped on that tiger shark's back and rode it across the deck like Cap'n Ahab rode the whale. Then Cap'n Peleg, he comes at that shark with a rifle and pumps hot lead into that beastie. Spittin' blood through his nasty teeth, that old tiger shark eats his way through the starboard side and dives into the water, me just a-huggin' his dorsal fin."

By now the three cats had reached another intersection where tourists played the curbside crawl. Across the street old Murdoch's, the island's ancient tourist shop, jutted over the warm Gulf waters and beckoned landlubbers to spend their dollars on imported sand dollars. A cigar store pirate lounged in an overstuffed rattan chair and fixed blank eyes on half-naked pedestrians.

"Underwater we was, that striped beastie leakin' blood like a sieve, and the water bubbles from his plunge ticklin' me whiskers. Just when I thinks this is me last ride, that shark thrashes to the surface and heads straight for Cap'n's ship. Believe me, I ain't never seen the likes of that tiger shark, and I sailed the Seven Seas and seen the Golden Cats of Zanzibar."

"H-how did you lose your leg, Chester?" purred Miss Panders.

"Ah, the leg! That tiger shark, he cruised for that ship like some kind of toothy torpedo, and cap'n, he's just a-clippin' away at 'em. Ten feet afore he slams jaws-first into the side, he puts on the fin brakes and I slides off him like a skippin' stone. I struggles to grab Cap'n Peleg's outstretched hand before that mad shark can turn 'round and get me. Just as I gets pulled clear of the water, that tiger shark leaps straight out of the briny depths, clamps down on me back hind leg, and clean bites it off. 'Course I yell like a sick lion, and cap'n, he pulls me to his chest."

Chester paused to relight his pipe. Miss Panders stood, mouth nearly touching her front paws, on the curb.

"And now comes the most incredible part of the story, Miss Panders. See, I was so dadblamed angry at that shark for cripplin' me that I tried to leap back into the water and duke it out with that old jaw bones."

Ninja Jules sneered. "I can see that one in technicolor. You fighting hungry tiger shark—UNDERWATER!"

Chester snorted and pipe smoke rose like a cloud over his head. "Would have too. But Cap'n Peleg, he holds me over the water, usin' me for bait, and that shark circlin' closer and closer, and Cap'n hollerin,' 'Come and get it, sharkie, nice fresh cat, come and get it!' and all the time he's got his rifle cocked and ready. When the shark leaps out of the water to get the rest of me, Cap'n, he blows daylight into that fish, and when it slammed into the water for the last time, that tiger shark landed in three or four meaty chunks. We did the shark, mates, we DID the shark."

Miss Panders just shook her dainty whiskers from side to side. Ninja Jules licked his eyebrow whiskers and pretended boredom. "Say, Chester. I thought you said cat-eating shark was great white shark that swallow right hind leg last time I hear story. Now it tiger shark bite off left hind leg. What really happen to leg? Ambulance run over it while you pass out on street?"

Chester gasped and pipe smoke curled from his nostrils. While he heaved for air, Miss Panders laughed and laughed. Then, her eyes full of tears, she said, "You tomcats. Don't you ever give it up? Come on now, no fighting. We're going to be late for Great-Aunt Meowkin's Reunion."

Ninja Jules took Chester, who was still wheezing for air, around the old cat's short-haired shoulder and good-naturedly growled, "Yeah, Miss Panders right. We get to reunion early, maybe some kitties there who not hear tiger shark story more than once. Just keep practicing limp, old sea cat."

Chester hissed at Ninja Jules, but then saw that the Korat was smiling and offering his paws, so the old Havana Brown tapped out his pipe and gimped along the street with all the aristo-catic swagger three good legs could muster.

Chapter Eight:

Percey and Evelyn on the Rocks

Like granite peninsulas the massive granite blocks stretch into the Gulf and partition the golden brown sands of Galveston Beach. Sunburned bathers with scarlet backs, fly fishermen with more bait than luck, and rubberneck tourists drawn to the sousing spray of the deep stand here and gaze out at the ocean and ponder the secrets beneath the waves.

And here where beach and boulder merge in the shadows of the seawall rest two enormously fat, blue-haired Chartreux cats sunning themselves in the afternoon salt air. Percey and Evelyn, Great-Aunt Meowkin's caretakers in her declining years, had annually hosted the reunion for the dear old girl. Bachelor toms, Percey and Evelyn had for several years enjoyed cream in imported saucers from the back door of the Bishop's Palace.

True aristo-cats, Percey and Evelyn had had a Parisian fling with the Episcopalians, but when the Catholic bishop expressed an interest in Vatican-trained felines, Percey and Evelyn materialized on the back step and meowed in Latin. In no time they knew their way around the old mansion and, having convinced the kitchen staff that they were authentic attack cats, were permitted to ride in the dumbwaiter when the bishop rang for a midnight snack of herrings and cream.

But when the bishop one day unexpectedly sailed to the Other Shore, the new landlords took a dim view of over-stuffed cats lounging on the velvet furniture and so Percey and Evelyn were shown the back door. For years the hefty Chartreux had run a rodent extermination business behind the warehouses in The Strand district, but advancing age had slowed the old toms to a crawl.

Nowadays Percey and Evelyn were professional caterers, providing the food and drink for party cats. As they had been Great-Aunt Meowkin's personal attendants, the task of preparing the reunion dinner naturally fell to them. Each year the hot gossip from the clipper ship ELISSA all the way to the toll bridge at San Luis Pass, a distance of thirty miles, was how Percey and Evelyn would outdo themselves at this year's reunion.

Last year the Galveston Cats had feasted on flounder fillets and tender chunks of sea bass. This year, the cats agreed, would top even turtle soup. What none of the arriving guests knew was that Percey and Evelyn had not a whiff of an idea what to serve at this year's reunion.

Yawning until his mouth resembled an open manhole with teeth, Percey licked his smokey blue fur and when it glistened, he spat out a nasty little hair ball.

"Evelyn, old boy, what shall we do for this year's reunion?" Percey smacked his lips as though the very air contained droplets of cream.

Evelyn stretched himself full length on the mica-speckled boulder and stared up at Percey through slitted eyes. "Do you mind, old top. I was taking a cat nap to get through to this evening when I plan to take a longer cat nap."

Percey tugged at his shag of fur and sniffed the air. "I say, there's a smell of shrimp in the air that positively rouses the taste buds. Come along now, Evelyn. Rise and shine and let's stir about. The company will be coming in a few hours."

Evelyn made clawing motions in the air and finally righted his bulk into a sitting position. Resting his large haunches on a boulder and allowing his glorious tail free rein over the side, Evelyn yawned tremendously and then he too sniffed the inviting air.

"Say, old bean, you're right. There is an overpowering aroma of shrimp coming from that rock jetty yonder." And he hiked his glorious plume of a tail over his head and pointed it due south.

"That puts me in the mood to tell another chapter in my life history," purred Percey.

"Oh bother with your autobiography, Percey," huffed Evelyn. "Don't try to impress me with your travels around the world. I'm not the bishop."

"More's the pity," sniffed Percey. "If you were, my book would be appearing in all the fine gift shops on The Strand. But if you promise not to interrupt me again, I MAY

69

permit you to hear the story of my youthful days aboard the good ship APRIL GALE as we sailed around Cape Horn to Cape Cod in the summer of '72."

"If I promise not to interrupt, does that mean you shall prepare dinner for our guests?" Evelyn asked, licking a stray hair into place.

"We'll both prepare the evening repast, and you shall listen, thank you. Now then. Back in '72, it was novel thinking for a ship's captain to take a cat aboard on an extended cruise. But I have no doubts that Cap'n Bob knew about my pedigree and my royal connections. You see, Evelyn, my grandfather guarded the Sultan's harem."

"To keep the mice in or the rats out?" Evelyn smirked.

"Be still and listen! Ah! That summer I was no more than a kitten, something like the feline cabin boy. Besides keeping the ship free of rodents, I helped the cook in the kitchen making pies and cakes and one-holers...."

Evelyn stopped his bathing to interrupt. "What in the name of Louis XVI are one-holers, old beret?"

"Oh pooh, Evelyn. Haven't you ever heard of doughnuts called one-holers. No, old fellow? Well, this cook was a mighty clever lad and above anything else he prized his naps. Do you begin to surmise a connection, Evelyn?"

"Don't get catty, please Percey," hissed Evelyn.

"So one fine morning while the ship was making ten knots about eighty miles southwest of Cape Cod, he whispers his plan to me. Would I help him catch a fine mess of shrimp for the Cap'n's table? He easily convinced me of the wisdom of his plan. All I had to do was sit in the stern of the ship and watch the nets that he had secured. Since everyone was up to their elbows in chores, no one bothered with a small smokey blue kitten lounging by the end of the boat."

"Well, don't leave me hanging like a hooked whiting, Percey. What happened?" Evelyn pretended interest.

"Certainly, old whistle. Come evening, the Cap'n and his first mate were down in his cabin smoking cigars and talking the way humans do. Presently I see the cook slip out of a doorway and tiptoe over to the nets. He gives me a pat on the head and asks how the shrimping is going. Naturally I have no idea, but I smile like I just swallowed a yellow canary. Then he commences to pull and heave and tug at the nets but they won't budge."

"So did you leap into action, old boy?" Evelyn licked a barnacle off his glorious tail.

"Indubitably, old snuffer. I had myself an inspiration. If the ship was cleaning the ocean floor of shrimp, and that's what was making the nets so heavy, then maybe if the ship came to a complete stop, why then, we could pull up the nets. So I dashed into the control room, yanked the throttle with my glorious tail, and pulled for every minnow of my worth."

Eyes raised, Evelyn sniffed, "Oh my, Percey. With your glorious tail, no less. Then what happened?"

Percey yowled like a tiger. "The same thing that we are about to do now. When the ship lurched to a stop, the nets were flung over on the deck and thousands and thousands of shrimp rained down on the astonished captain and crew. Why, the ship was ankle-deep in the little pink morsels, and we took in three thousand pounds of the crunchy crustaceans."

"And what happened to the cook, Percey, old top hat."

"Oh, that's the best part, old slouch hat. The cook became something of a hero when we reached Cape Cod. Cap'n Bob offered to double his wages, but the cook took his share of the shrimp and opened up a chowder bar right on the docks. Seems to me he retired a few years ago when the last of his shrimp disappeared down some Yankee's gullet in Martha's Vineyard."

Eveyln seemed genuinely impressed. Then he raised one golden eye and asked, "Percey, that's an AWFUL lot of shrimp to make chowder out of for all those years!"

But Percey was already whispering a plan of action to his bachelor friend. "When I rake that fisherman's legs, you steal his bait bucket. Then meet me here under the seawall."

Evelyn protested. "But Percey, we'll need more than ONE bait bucket to feed all the Galveston Cats!"

But Percey was already mincing his way up the rock jetty, sniffing into the yawning cracks between the boulders and dodging the spray that splashed the rocks and ran down the sides in tiny rivulets.

"Hey, old whiskers, wait for Evelyn," the large Chartreux yowled, marching after the smokey blue furball swaying pendulum-like on the wet rocks.

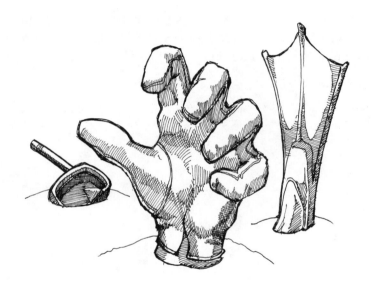

Chapter Nine:

Percey and Evelyn Go Beachcombing

Four buckets of blood bait and one long sustained fur-bath later, two plump, elderly smokey blue cats waddled down the empty beach. Out in the Gulf chugged three ancient shrimpers, closely followed by a living spiral of seagulls.

"Nasty buggers," growled Percey. "Always looking for a handout. Those birds would steal pennies off your dead granny's eyes if they got half a chance," he continued, dragging a half-empty, blood-stained bucket behind him.

"I say, old nipper," complained Evelyn. "That's exactly what we've been doing for the past hour. I don't know about you, Percey, but I'm not ready to become crab bait when some outraged fisherman sees us stealing his bucket." Evelyn's paws gripped a groaning bucket filled with bait shrimp and squid.

"Oh bother, Evelyn. No fisherman is going to make crab canapés out of us. Why, that last fellow just felt like chasing us down the jetty with his rod and reel to frighten us," Percey persisted.

"Easy for you to say, Percey. He wasn't whipping your flanks and screaming 'Crab bait! Crab bait!' for nothing," snarled Evelyn.

"Let's forget raiding fishermen's bait buckets and concentrate on finding paw snacks on the beach," Percey said. "On any given day just about anything may float to shore on Galveston Island."

Eveyln stopped to moisten his whiskers and take a deep breath from toting the bucket. "You can certainly say that again, Percey. Say, old mouser, here's a perfectly good mullet in the surf. Let me pitch him in your bucket, and you carry the provisions for awhile."

Percey watched as Evelyn rattled the cold fish home. Between kitty licks on his glorious tail, Evelyn asked, "Have I ever told you about the strangest beach-combing adventure I have ever had?"

Cocking his ears, Percey sniffed a story. "Why no, Evelyn, I don't believe you have. Why don't you recite your adventure while we prowl the beach for party favors."

"Oh quite," sniffed Evelyn. Stooping over to examine an odd piece of driftwood, Evelyn remarked, "Oh, let's keep this piece, Percey. It's shaped just like the lifeguard over at Stewart Beach." He held up a thick, smooth chunk of wood that resembled a tirejack.

"Oh yes, the very thing," smirked Percey. "But don't fill my bucket with pieces of wood. Look, Evelyn! A pair of shrimper's gloves."

Two watersoaked latex gloves lay in a heap atop a tangled mass of rust-colored seaweed. Perhaps it was the onrush of the tide, or a sailor's whim, or maybe it was the inspiration of the Old Man of the Sea; no matter, the gloves were joined at the rubbery fingers in twisted knots.

"The very thing, old sea horse," cackled Evelyn. "Let me share my adventure with you, Percey. As the two well-fed cat-erer cousins trekked across the beach, a solitary seagull swooped low over the water, dived into the blue water, and emerged moments later with a flapping fish in its beak.

"Now Percey, remember the weekend that you and the bishop journeyed over to Port Bolivar for a picnic?" asked Evelyn.

"Of course, old crown," beamed Percey. "The Bishop packed a huge picnic basket of goodies—snapper filets, cat-fish nuggets and tasty crab claws—for an afternoon repast. We were gone all day and just made the last ferry ride across the channel."

"The very same. After you departed, I dined on kippers and cream, and then decided to take a morning stroll near the west end of the island, out past where Fort Crockett was once headquartered on the beach head. I took a small walking stick with me just in case some oyster lad late for school might be stirring in the sands."

Something white glittered in the surf, and when Evelyn reached down to seize it, he whistled, "What luck, Percey! A complete sand dollar."

"Lucky you, Evelyn," replied Percey. "All I have in my bucket is spare change fragments. But do go on, Evelyn."

Evelyn daintily stepped over a puddle of jellyfish rotting on the beach and continued. "Not a hundred feet down the beach I discovered a pair of rubber gloves very like the ones we saw back there. The gloves had HANDS in them!"

Percey stopped and swallowed hard and his eyes bulged like he was choking on a catfish bone. "H-human hands, Evelyn?"

"Oh, quite, quite. Believe me, Percey, the breakfast rose up in me like smoke up a chimney. I poked at the gloves and disturbed a whole family of loathsome sand crabs enjoying lunch on the beach."

Percey grimaced, but still had the presence of mind to hook a large blue crab resting upside down on the beach and flip it into his bucket. "Pray continue, Evelyn."

"I struck out boldly again, fearing that I had not seen the last of such gruesome terrors. And I was right! Another fifty steps brought me paw to claw with a large black flipper, the kind underwater divers use. Cautiously, I turned it over and the hair stood up on my spine! Percey, inside the flipper was—A HUMAN FOOT!"

Percey's eyes bulged and his breath came in fitful gasps."A...a real human foot, Evelyn?"

78

"Oh yes, yes. Now I had found a pair of hands and a foot, complete with five toes and part of a leg. The part missing, I'm afraid to say, dear Percey, had been neatly severed to the bone."

But poor Percey swooned and would have fallen like a block of granite had not Evelyn caught the fainting tom in his hairy blue arms. Momentarily, Percey's eyes fluttered and his sea legs returned.

"Whew, that's ghastly, Evelyn. Certainly you didn't find anything else spewed up on the beach?"

Evelyn slowly shook his head. "Oh no, Percey. The worst is yet to come. No more than twenty-five feet from where I had found the black flipper and human foot, I spied a round black object half-hidden in the sand."

"Was...it human?" Percey quavered.

"Holding my breath, I poked around the thing, knocking off the stubborn sand until I shook with fear. It was an underwater diver's cap and goggles! I stared and stared at that cap until I noticed little twisters of sand corkscrewing like crazy. Very, very slowly I lifted the cap and there, to my disgust and amazement, was a HUMAN HEAD!" Evelyn paused to watch Percey collapse in a heap on the damp sand.

When Percey awoke some minutes later, he saw through slitted eyes that Evelyn was enjoying the last of the drowned crabs. "Hey, old sport! Those crabs are for the guests."

"Of course, of course. But I became famished, dear Percey, what with waiting around for you to wake up and wanting to finish my story."

"You mean to tell me that's not all of it? You find a pair of gloves with human hands tied into knots, a flipper with a severed foot and leg, and then a human head intact inside a diver's cap. And that's not ALL?" Percey was huffing and puffing excitedly.

Evelyn licked a front paw and combed his curling side whiskers. "No, not all. You see, old boy, the little clouds of sand were caused by the palpitating head. When I roused enough courage to tug the head out of the muck, I went eyeball to eyeball with the diver himself. Suddenly the eyes of the diver blinked and without so much as a please and thank you, the diver ups and asks me would I kindly collect the rest of him and stitch him back together with seaweed and ship's rope."

Percey snorted and stamped a heavy paw into the sand. "Oh, you awful storyteller, you. Do you REALLY expect me to believe such a yarn as that, Evelyn?"

"Eveyln giggled like a tickled chipmunk. "Great sea urchins, Percey! I don't believe half of it myself."

Both cats fell on the beach and rolled in throes of laughter. Then they commenced washing the sand from their glorious tails. Between kitty licks, Percey had to ask, "Did you stitch the diver back into some semblance of humanity, Evelyn?"

"Oh bother, Percey. If you want to go see the lad, why he's waiting tables at the Ocean Grill. Just one thing, Percey. His head bobs up and down when he serves you." Evelyn watched Percey's facial expression change from curiosity to outrage. "Here," Evelyn said, shoving a bucket of writhing bait fish into Percey's blue midriff. "give the old heave-ho to this pail of paw snacks. We want to serve our guests a splendid repast, you know, old rat chaser."

"I know who I'd like to give the old heave-ho to," hissed Percey under his breath. But he picked up the bucket of fish hors d'oeuvres and followed the swaying pendulum of Evelyn's smokey blue rump down the beach to the place where the Galveston Cats would break a flounder for Great-Aunt Meowkin's Reunion.

Chapter Ten:

Pyewackit Swims the Deep

"Flounder?"

Pyewackit interrupted cleaning her whiskers of the last drop of cream and frowned at Tabitha as she fished in her purse for the car keys. "I thought you said we were leaving now for the reunion, and now you tell me we have to shop for flounder. I just don't understand human pets sometimes." The little white kitten sniffed wetly through pink nostrils to show her irritation.

"Oh, stop snorting like a puffer fish, Pyewackit. You know we can't just appear at Great-Aunt Meowkin's Reunion without the proper party snacks. And we have to bring the flounder to break with the Galveston Cats tonight. We are honoring the memory of Great-Aunt Meowkin and Winnie, remember, fuzz ball?"

In response, Pyewackit stuck out her little pink tongue. "Oh, all right, Tabitha. I'm just along for the ride. But where are you going to find flounders at this time of the day. All these restaurants are serving shrimp po-boys."

Tabitha whisked her dear kitten into the bulging purse and sailed on long skirts into the busy street where she deposited her furry package in the front seat of the old Volvo. "Let's drive over to the channel fish market, Pyewackit, and find our flounders." And with that, Tabitha cranked up the ancient import and tootled down Market Street to 19th Street, passing the large brick Peanut Butter Warehouse and a half-filled parking lot. There, a ruined brick chimney stood silent sentinel over sweating motorists searching for a free parking spot.

Pyewackit peeped out of the purse and shook her whiskers. "Where are we now, Tabitha? You move faster than an electric eel when you're on a tight schedule, do you know that? Say, where are we going to buy the flounder?" As the Volvo rattled over the railroad tracks and entered the Pier 19 parking lot, Pyewackit's blue eyes rested on a two-story restaurant and a snug little row of fish market shops. In the distance the island's mosquito shrimp boats lay at anchor.

The parking lot in front of the Pier 19 restaurant was full, and yet as the creaking old Volvo drove up, a brown van loaded with kids pulled out from a tight parking spot and Tabitha wheeled in and stopped at the entrance to the island's oldest fish market.

"Did you hear what that man said to his boys, Tabitha?" Pyewackit's tiny ears were alert. "He said, 'Do you think we have enough shrimp for a family feast?' What if they don't sell flounder here, Tabitha?"

But Tabitha was already out of the car, purse in hand, and marching into the teeming market. "Hush, Pyewackit, and learn to visualize."

84

The little fish market was a snug, open-air shop with a back door that emptied into the channel. Sun-baked, grizzled shrimpers who rose with the midnight tides searched the brown waters for a day's worth of fishes: mullet, sheep's head, ocean trout, red snapper, blue crabs, and fat pink shrimp. Long before the shorts-clad tourists were awake, these veterans of the shrimp wars had sold their bounty to the market's swarthy owners, who iced the haul in big metal buckets and all the livelong day they filleted fish for the dinner table.

A bold young man who might have been LaFitte's man-at-arms in another time asked Tabitha what looked appetizing, and the red-haired granddaughter of Winnie asked for four flounders.

"So sorry, lady," said the youth with dancing eyes. "We sold the last one to a bearded fellah from Dallas."

Tabitha smiled and nodded at the ice-filled bucket. "Perhaps you should look again, young man. I see four tasty flatheads right there."

To the young man's astonishment, there lay on the icy table four perfect little flounders. "Why, I could have sworn..."

"Never swear when you can simply visualize, darling," cooed Tabitha. "And I'd like those flounders packed in ice, please. My kitten and I have to drive over to the western end of the island this evening for a special reunion. Don't we, Pyewackit." Carefully lifting the small Siamese from her purse, Tabitha placed the curious kitten on the counter near an ice floe of red snappers. As the young man started to protest, Tabitha gave him a faraway glance and said, "Oh, don't worry, Pyewackit's a vegetarian."

When the wrapped flounders were paid for, Tabitha stroked the kitten's long white hair and said, "Now, I think we are ready for Great-Aunt Meowkin's Reunion. Are you ready to go, Pyewackit?"

But Pyewackit was sniffing at the cold flanks of a filleted ocean trout and thinking maybe she was hungry again for kitty snacks. "Where do they get all these tasty fish, Tabitha? This is an ocean of goodies. Meow!"

Tabitha smiled. "Shall we visualize and find out, Pyewackit? See that shrimp boat docked at the pier there? Look at those nets! Now visualize, little fish, and swim with me."

Pyewackit closed her blue eyes and visualized herself swimming through the murky brown waters. Beside her finned a larger fish like herself, and the two red snappers swam for deeper waters.

Ohhh, what a rush of air bubbles, thought Pyewackit as she fishtailed beyond the danger of the shrimpers' nets. Gradually the ocean floor came into view, an immense underwater desert of rippled sand and wavy dune. Here and there shells of different sizes glittered in the half-light and dancing anemone tentacles teased innocent blue fins. Pyewackit pecked at the underwater vegetation and was about to sample a fat pink worm when Tabitha nudged her with a powerful fin thrust.

"Silly minnow! That's no worm, Pyewackit, that's the tongue of a huge sea turtle. Watch!" Tabitha made as though to nibble the curvaceous morsel when the giant jaws clamped shut. Pyewackit's scales trembled with fear.

"Oh, thank you, Tabitha. That mean old turtle would have made a canapé of me. Say, look at that cave over there!"

Pyewackit swam furiously to an underwater rock cairn dripping with evil-looking seaweed. "What if there's buried treasure here, Tabitha? Or maybe a treasure chest of Spanish gold just waiting to be unlocked. Let's explore, Tabitha." And saying that, Pyewackit began to poke, nose-first, into the nooks and crannies of the heap of rocks.

Quicker than thought, a great, green, one-eyed moray eel shot out of one of the dark holes, savage teeth snapping like castanets. The hideous monster barely missed the frantic little snapper and it whirled on one dorsal fin and whipped around the mouldering heap of stones with the eel's slathering jaws snapping hotly behind her.

"Help, Tabitha!" bubbled the terrified little fish. "I'm going to be eaten by this slimy, snakey fish and I'm supposed to eat them. Help!"

Faster and faster the little snapper and the great, green, one-eyed moray eel swam around and between the algae-covered rocks, and closer and closer slashed the dreaded teeth. Pyewackit, in a whirr of air bubbles, dived into one of the dark caverns—too late!—it was a dead end, and the snakey monster whiplashed furiously toward the the trembling snapper, gaping mouth wide open for the kill.

"Tabitha, where are you?" the little snapper gurgled, closing its eyes as the white jaws of death breathed a hot stench of rotting fish on Pyewackit. "I never want to play snapper again, do you hear me, Tabitha!"

The menacing teeth came closer, closer, and Pyewackit felt a terrible pinching, a painful toothy clamping on her extremities and she yowled like a she-panther for her human pet and she opened her eyes and there stood Tabitha, smiling down at her mischieviously.

"Dear kitten, what has attached itself to your glorious tail?" Tabitha asked the terrified, wide-eyed little Siamese.

And there, one blue claw waving in the air and the other menacing poor Pyewackit's white frizzed tail, dangled a large blue crab. Tabitha unplucked the frisky crab and cuddled her shaking kitten.

"That wasn't funny at all, Tabitha and I'm mad at you for visualizing that I was a little snapper about to be eaten by a great, green, one-eyed moray eel." Pyewackit climbed quickly onto Tabitha's shoulder where she stood, back arched and tail electrified, for all the world looking like a witch's broom cat.

"Ohh, did my little kitten become scared of a tiny crab with wee claws? You have to be careful when you visualize, darling. Sometimes you may not like what you see." Tabitha cuddled her purring friend who now burrowed deeply into the red-haired woman's arms.

Together they left the fish market and over the voices of hungry tourists, a young man hollered, "Hey lady! You forgot your flounders," He held up a plump bag dripping with melting ice.

"Not at all, young man. They're already in my car, thank you." Tabitha made a face at the puzzled boy who looked in the bag, expecting to see glassy-eyed flatheads, and stared instead at a mess of soggy jumbo shrimp.

"Well, I'll be a salty dog," whistled the young man, looking at the bag's contents and back at the bumper sticker on the disappearing Volvo. From the backseat window a tiny Siamese kitten waved a white paw and gnawed on a crab claw.

Chapter Eleven:

Winnie Walks the Beach at Sunset

A ll the way up 24th Street chugged the trusty Volvo, past the weathered statues of war heroes and mom and pop stores, through the little neighborhoods where Victorian mansions rose imperiously over the roofs of clapboard shacks and the palm-lined streets overshadowed the flowering hibiscus hedges.

"I wonder if Odacious will be here this evening?" asked Tabitha, dodging a black kitten foraging for oyster po-boy tidbits on the ground near a bloated trash can.

From the back window came a growly voice. "Why did we have to buy flounders, Tabitha?" Pyewackit worried a crab claw and sucked on the sweet flesh.

"You haven't heard the story of my grandmother Winnie who walked the beach at sunset the night of the Great Storm? Oh, Pyewackit, it is a tale to tell. Come sit up here in the front seat with me and curl in my lap and I'll share the secret why the Galveston Cats break a flounder every year on the night of September 8th."

"And no more visualizing, please Tabitha," asked the little kitten as she made a nest in her human pet's lap and made biscuits with her pushing, pulling wee claws.

"All right," laughed the gifted woman. "Just listen!"

The old Volvo stopped at the traffic light on Seawall Boulevard and Tabitha gazed out at the wide expanse of the Texas Gulf. For just a second she seemed mesmerized by its beauty and then she gasped as the memories lodged in her throat.

"That night before the Great Storm, Winnie and her brothers and sisters were out there, somewhere, running up and down the beach, chasing each other and diving into the waves. Winnie was the youngest, and her brothers used to pick on her, throwing her into the surf and dumping wet mud on her head, and when she had had enough, she quietly slipped away and walked the beach by herself."

The light changed to green and Tabitha turned right onto the Seawall and drove past the island's breezy shade and t-shirt shops.

"Of course, the seawall and this road didn't exist in 1900, the year the Great Storm destroyed most of the humans and cats on Galveston Island. The seawall was built much later, and the Army Corps of Engineers had something to do with its construction. And so did Winnie and Great-Aunt Meowkin, as you shall hear tonight, little missy. Are you asleep, already?"

Pyewackit opened one blue eye to a slit and shook her pretty white head. "Please go on. I'm listening."

"That night was calm enough. Bathers in long swimsuits prowled the beach. Men smoked cigars and women sipped lemonade in tall glasses. Children played in the waves or made sand castles on the beach. There were a few scattered clouds in the sky and a light southwesterly wind, just like any late summer evening in Galveston.

"Winnie had walked down the beach, carrying a little sand bucket with her to play beachcomber. She loved finding unusual-looking shells and driftwood, and she especially liked sand dollars. As she waded in the ankle-deep waters, she made an amazing discovery. She found a little flounder in a tidal pool, and the poor thing was gasping its life away!

"Now my grandmother Winnie loved animals and it broke her heart to see that little fish die on the beach. So she scooped it up in her hands and when she threw it back into the waves, an astonishing thing happened. The flounder swam back to the shore and tried to wriggle its way into the damp sand.

"Winnie had never seen anything like it before. Fish, she reasoned, needed water to survive. And yet this little flounder risked dying on dry land just to burrow deeper into the sand. Winnie couldn't understand why her fish would want to hide, but that's exactly what the goggle-eyed flathead was doing. Then the moment seized her.

"The wind picked up out of the east. At first, it was just a gentle swell and a few white clouds streaking in from the sea. As Winnie watched, the waves began to froth and writhe in white foam, whipped on by the increasing winds. The little flounder had disappeared in the damp sand by now and the wind began to whistle and the smell of rain was in the air. Dark, rumbling clouds suddenly appeared over the eastern end of the island and the winds continued to blow.

"In her heart Winnie sensed the disaster. This was no summer squall headed for the island. She could see people playing on the beach, unconcerned about the approaching storm. Even when the waves became choppy and angrily slapped the beach, boys and men calmly stood in the surf and fished. Winnie felt the temperature drop and the sudden chill frightened her.

"Then she realized why the little flounder had hidden itself in the sand. It was trying to escape the storm, to ride out the howling winds and deadly waves. Winnie looked out at the wind-whipped Gulf and saw a vision that terrified her: waves fifteen feet high sweeping over the island, destroying everything in its wake; winds screaming and tearing at roofs and telephone wires; rain in sheets swallowing homes and buildings; angry waters, churning, boiling, brown waters consuming everything in sight; an island submerged under the hammer blows of a great hurricane.

"Winnie heard on the winds a man's fearful voice alerting sunbathers to leave the beach and seek shelter in their homes, a frightened voice that appealed to reason and urged everyone to run, run for their lives before the waves washed them away.

"She ran as fast as she could back to where her brothers and sisters were playing, but they were nowhere to be found. They had become panic-stricken by the howling storm and dashed for the safety of home. Winnie realized she was alone on the beach and the great roaring of the wind and waves was her only companion. Terrified, she wailed for her mother but the great storm swelled in intensity and giant waves pounded the beach, and the swirling waters flooded the streets.

"As the giant waves rolled over the beach, a frightened little girl, my grandmother Winnie, made a mad dash for cover in an empty wooden building. The streets were deserted and the rains rattled the windows. Winnie looked out the cracked glass pane and shuddered as the winds howled outside. Then an enormous wave slammed against the building and it leaned heavily on one side and collapsed in the raging waters.

"And that is all Winnie remembered about the Great Storm that swept over this tiny island. The waves rose four feet in four seconds, Pyewackit. Don't you wish you could visualize that, little missy?"

But Pyewackit was sound asleep, visions of kitty snacks leaping like ocean trout in the tidal pools of her mind. Tabitha stroked the sleeping kitten and stared hard at the calm waters of the Gulf. Sighing, she said in a quiet voice, "Winnie, I don't know how you and Great-Aunt Meowkin survived that monstrous hurricane. But I'm happy that you did because I have the memories in my heart. I know what you went through, dearest Winnie.

After all, it was you who taught me how to visualize the moment. And tonight, we break a flounder, the same fish that once warned you of the Great Storm, in your honor and in memory of those who went before us to the Other Shore."

Out in the calm waters a black fin suddenly pitched forward and disappeared. "And there were no dolphins that day to save even a kitten like you, Pyewackit," whispered Tabitha.

A hundred yards farther out in the Gulf two tiny figures on surf boards danced on the waves and sped towards the beach now crowded with well-oiled tourists broiling like lobsters in the afternoon sun.

Chapter Twelve:

One-Eyed Tom and the Devil Fish

B lustery days when the winds whip the waves into heaving breakers that pound the rock jetties and shake the fishing piers rouse an unusual species of bathers. Brown as cinnamon and fearless of undertows, they paddle out beyond the breakers seeking glory, even redemption, for the sin of being terrestrial.

In rainbow wet suits that seem painted on strong torsos and thighs, they pursue the zigzag line of churning water, praying for that supreme moment when board and wave are one. Of all the creatures of the sea, none is more insatiable than the tribe of surfers famished for one more miraculous walk on the water astride a smooth waxed board.

As One-Eyed Tom gimped down the beach, still chuckling at how he had turned the buckets on those two overstuffed cats, Rumpy and Stumpy, his good eye caught two young felines fighting the waves out past the peeling remnants of the old Balinese Club.

"Young whippercats," One-Eyed Tom muttered to himself. "Think that just 'cause they can dance on a piece of plywood, they can waltz on the water. Durn croaker heads."

The old crabber watched in amazement as the two chocolate glossy cats raced along the breaker line, crouched low on their boards and outraced the foaming waters to within yards of the shore. Then, like aroused seals, they plunged into the froth and churn, and carried their boards onto the beach where they planted them in the wet sand.

One-Eyed Tom yowled after them, "Not bad navigatin' for a cupple landlubbers!" The two surfing cats turned and hissed at the old crabber, but he only laughed and slapped a bony knee.

"Rest easy, lads. No hard feelin's. My name's One-Eyed Tom, the crab cat. What your names, mateys?"

The younger cats sniffed and stretched on the damp beach. "His name be Nibs. I be Nubs. We Jamaican surf-cats come to U.S. to dig the waves and dance 'round a bonfire wid some wild kitties. Why you no dig surfin'?" growled Nubs.

"Belay that nonsense, my hearties. I'm the ring-tailed tooter when it come to surfin'. Fact is," and One-Eyed Tom puffed out his glorious tail, "I come close to inventin' surfin' in these waters."

The two Burmese shorthairs, their dreadlocks stiff with mud and pieces of shell, meowed like lovesick toms on a backyard fence.

One-Eyed Tom glared at the cats rolling on the brown sand and when their laughter died down, he said sternly, "Avast there, mateys! Come to starboard and anchor down. I said I been a-surfin' in my prime, long before youse pussycats got yer patties wet with mamma's milk."

Both surfing cats shook their ebony curls and stared at the old cat, who stood there staring at them, tail twitching for a fight and the patch over the right eye flying a pirate skull and crossbones.

"Easy, ole cat," smirked Nibs. "We no diss ya. In Jamaica plenty old cats go surf de big waves. Some, dey even come back to tell 'bout it."

"Das rite," chimed in Nubs. "Our daddy, he was champine surfer in he time. Won many, many trophies. All kitties on island friend to Daddy. Ain't dat rite, Nibs?"

Nibs nodded and asked, "So tell us surfin' cats 'bout yo surfin' days, ole cat. Ever see shark in water? In Jamaica big hammerheads, bigger den yacht. Surf cats see black fin, dey paddle back to shore plenty quick."

One-Eyed Tom sat on his haunches and laughed. "Hammerheads, nothing. Just a big fish, mateys. Didja ever see a devil fish afore?"

Both Nibs and Nubs looked blankly at their interrogator and slowly shook their wet whiskers. "What you mean, ole cat, by devil fish?" asked Nubs. "What is devil fish?"

Looking out at the Gulf where a single seagull, framed by the setting sun, streaked across the horizon, One-Eyed Tom lounged on the beach and said, "Now listen, me true crew, just ye dry off a spell and let me regale ye young surf cats with the true tale how I invented surfin' in these parts AND battled with the evil devil fish."

Nibs and Nubs grunted and began slowly to dry themselves off with sandpaper tongues. As the old crabber began his story, the two Jamaican cats dried and chewed their fur. Apologetically, Nibs said by way of explanation, "We surf cats sleep on beach at night and in morning our bodies crawlin' wid ancestors."

Nodding, One-Eyed Tom made a mental note that in the Caribbean, sand fleas were called ancestors. Tearing a chew from his plug, OLD MORRIS, the one-time first mate on H.M.S. PITTYS commenced his tale.

"Back in '76, I think it was, Cap'n Bildad calls us on deck and gives us the bad news. He's quittin' the deep-sea fishin' business for good. Got too old, bones ache in stormy weather, wants to run a grog shop on land. So he gives each crewman his wages and tells 'em he can have a memento from the ship. Some of them cats took first one thing and then another, and when it comes me turn, I looks Cap'n Bildad in the eyes—I had both eyes then, mateys—and asks for the lifeboat hooked to the lee side."

One-Eyed Tom paused to shift his chew and see if the two surfing cats were still listening.

"Go on, ole cat," said Nibs. "We can bathe and listen at same time."

"So Cap'n Bildad gives me the little skiff, and was I pleased with meself. I was the only cat on the island with his own boat. Every morning before the sun peeked over the blue waves, I was rowin,' rowin,' into the deep waters where the fat tuna swim. I had rigged a little sail in the belly of the boat, so's when me paws begun to ache, I could let the wind take up the slack.

"All day I fish and me boat, she fills up with tasty mackerel and trout. One day I hook into a school of tuna, and it was 'Garfield, pass the lasagna' and them fish a-floppin' and tryin' to leap out of me boat and me a-poundin' them with the oar. I was so busy knockin' fish glassy-eyed, I never noticed two huge grey tentacles grippin' the bow."

Nibs spit out a hairball and stared at One-Eyed Tom. "Tentacles, ole cat? You be attacked by squid?"

The old crab cat paused and leaning back, arched a long stream of brown liquid into the sand. "Weren't no measly fishbait squid, matey. Was a devil fish. A giant octopus."

The mocha-hair cats stopped drying off and tugged at their dreadlocks. "Oh, you be jammin' wid octopus, ole cat?" asked Nubs. "Devil fish is octopus."

The old cat nodded and grinned. "And they be fearless of man or cat and they be HUNGRY. With one swipe of his tentacle, he grabbed me tuna and disappeared underwater. Now what was I gonna do, surf cats? That blamed devil fish had me tuna, and now he was a-comin' after me for dessert. I didn't wait for no invitation. I started a-rowin' like the Great Storm was a-blowin' fifteen foot waves at me. But that devil fish, he kept a-chargin' me. With each stroke of me oar, I could see him a-gainin', his ugly bald head a-pokin' through the water and his tentacles a-wavin' like angry snakes in the air."

"What did you do, ole cat?" asked Nubs.

"Yeah, and what 'bout de surfin'?" insisted Nibs. One-Eyed Tom shifted his cud and silenced the two surf cats with a quick paw. "Hold on, I'm comin' to that. With every stroke, that devil fish pulled at me boat and ripped a plank off. In seconds, water began a-spoutin' in half a dozen places in the bottom of me boat. Then it just caved in. Like this." And the old crabber, to illustrate his point, placed his paws together and then wriggled his claws apart slowly.

"I wasn't a-goin' to be no snack for that devil fish as long as I had breath in me ribs, so when I plunged into the water, I clawed at the sail and righted it and then heaved meself on two long pieces of wood. Then I takes a deep breath and blows for all me worth, and, surf cats, that sail, she begun a-billowin' and next thing I know, the sail catches the breeze, and I'm a-racin' back to shore with that devil fish just a-tearin' after me."

"You ride de waves on boat's ribs?" asked Nubs. "De planks, dey act like surfboard, right, ole cat?"

"Sure as youse sittin' here drippin' sea weed off yer tails, I did," insisted One-Eyed Tom. "When I was about three hundred yards from shore, I look behind me, thinkin' that devil fish lost interest in One-Eyed Tom, but no, he's still a-blowin' and a-goin'. His tentacles was mere inches from me tail, but, oh, the ride! The wind was a-blastin' me face and the cool spray was a-whistlin' round me whiskers. I tell you, surf cats, it was delirious a-ridin' them waves."

Nubs elbowed Nibs and together the two Jamaican cats laughed like longshoremen on Saturday night liberty. "Oh, we can see it now, ole cat. You ridin' the waves, and de devil fish bobbin' like great jellyfish in the surf," they yowled.

"Ye got that right. Just as the waves gave out and I was about to plunge into the water again, the devil fish wrapped one nasty tentacle 'round me and begun to pull me down. I thought I was one drowned cat for sure. But with me last ounce of strength, me hearties, I ran the pointy end of the sail into that ugly devil fish's yeller eye and suddenly the waves went inky. The devil fish, he let me go, and I floated ashore like driftwood. I was half-drowned and felt like piranhas was rippin' at me head, but I was alive, mateys. I was alive!"

For several moments neither of the surf cats spoke. Then Nubs asked, "Dat good tale, ole cat. Maybe you did bring surfin' to this island. Maybe you even fight de devil fish and live to tell de story. Dey just one ting."

One-Eyed Tom dug a little hole in the damp sand

105

with his hind paw, spat the chaw in the hole, and filled it with dirt. The two surfing cats had by now retrieved their boards and were waxing the surfaces. "What 'one ting' might that be, mateys?"

"How we know dat be true tale. No devil fish 'round here, no boat. No witnesses to de battle. How we know for sure?" Nibs looked at the old crabber with a smirk.

"Oh, is it proof ye want, is it? Why, just ye two Jamaican alley cats look at this!" And One-Eyed Tom peeled back the fur along his midsection to show an ancient wound that looked like a Harley had burned rubber on the pale skin.

"That's where the devil fish wrapped his tentacles around me and pulled me under. See that! There's the nasty critter's snaky signature burned into me belly! How's that fer proof?" he challenged the surfing cats who were now swimming, whiskers-deep, in the brown waters.

"Dat proof enuf fo me. You believe, Nubs?"

Nubs paddled on his board and nodded. "Yah. Ole cat, yo one lean, mean surfin' machine. Come to Jamaica, we tak yo to beach party and tell de story again. Yo have kitties want to share blanket wid yo 'till de fire goes out."

One-Eyed Tom watched as the two surf cats paddled out to where the breakers rolled relentlessly in a foaming, heaving motion as though the sea breathed waves. "Watch out for devil fish," the old crabber hollered.

Standing on their boards, the two grinning surf cats grinned and waved. Then they caught a good, long wave and walked on the water, fearless of the creatures of the deep.

Watching the two acrobatic cats frolic in the water, One-Eyed Tom gummed another chaw and yowled at the setting sun. "Guess I better shake a tail or I'll be late for Great-Aunt Meowkin's Reunion. Hope those two worthless caretakers of hers, Percey and Evelyn, don't serve up no blasted octopus. One mouthful of tentacles is enough for me for nine lifetimes."

And the old crab cat trotted down the beach, every now and then sniffing the remains of a rotting fish or scaring the scavenger crabs into the surf.

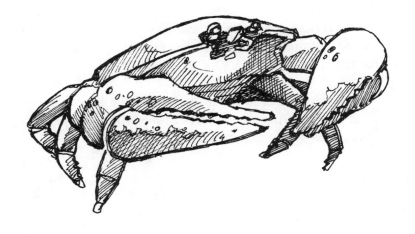

Chapter Thirteen:

Odacious Remembers Big Black Jack Johnson

U p 39th Street strolled the two black Bombay cats, past the rows of white clapboard houses where old black men sat and drank beer from paper sacks, past the tiny yards decorated with rows of pink and white oleanders and dripping wash on tippled clothesline poles, past ruined cars with open hoods parked on the cracked sidewalk, past weedy little parks enclosed in chain link fences where sweating sons of Africa played roundball, past little mom and pop stores with metal bars over the windows to discourage daylight robberies, past dark alleys and one-way streets cramped with the suffocating words, "No Exit."

Another Galveston lurks behind the boulevard stage props of condos and patio restaurants where the tourists play at vacation; between The Strand and the Seawall lies the real Galveston, home to working class heroes and drifters, Navy pensioners and widows, a Noah's Ark of humanity. And Galveston Cats.

The bigger of the ebony felines carried himself as befits a respected member of the cat community. Slow, easy walk and talk, that was Odacious. Tagging alongside him like a hungry kitten chasing a housewife 'round the kitchen for a saucer of cream skipped Presto. No bigger than a minute, Presto weaved in and out of the graceful strides of the larger cat. Every now and then Presto would whine, "How much longer, Odacious?"

Now Odacious never got in a hurry about anything, even eating. When Presto felt his taste buds Watusi in front of an open-air fish market, he begged Odacious to dash in and paw a mackerel, but Odacious only maintained his slow stroll. Patience, he reminded the hungry kitten, will fill a shrimpboat, but Haste won't tie the worm to a hook. Ain't gonna eat no worms, the kitten told himself, struggling to keep up with the proud black panther of a cat.

As they passed the Shrimp-n-Stuff restaurant on O Street, Presto could smell the fried fish cooking and he smacked his tiny lips.

"When we gonna get there, Odacious?" he meowed.

"In due time, little cat, in due time," came the measured answer.

"You been saying that since we left F Street, and I ain't seen fin nor claw of no reunion. Say, Odacious, I'm getting really hungry, how 'bout you?"

"Patience, Presto, patience. Have a workout with your patience. Go ten rounds with the Hungries and flatten 'em. Remember, little cat. Patience will catch a shrimp boat full...."

"Yeah, I know. And Haste won't drown a worm. But that don't help my tummy. How much longer we have to walk before we get to eat, Odacious?"

Odacious stopped and licked one glossy flank. Then he studied the kitten meowing fiercely at his feet. What a runt, he told himself. But I told his mamma I would raise him like my own son. And bless me for a sea snake, ain't nobody gonna stop me from keeping that vow. Smiling at Presto, the big cat said, "Look here, little cat. Follow my paw with your eyes up this street. When we runs out of street, we're there. Now, why don't you just punch out them Hungries, pound 'em into the street, and just keep up with me."

Presto nodded dutifully, but when Odacious wasn't looking, the kitten discovered the remnants of an oyster po-boy half-hidden in the weedy ditch. But before the kitten could swallow even a mouthful of tartar sauce, Odacious had grabbed Presto by the nape of the neck and shook him silly.

"Little cat, you in training now. Don't eat that trash. Someday you might just have to step into the ring and go ten rounds against Big Black Jack Johnson." Odacious dropped the starving kitten on the street and then stood on his tail so he couldn't lick the bread crumbs.

Looking up at the unsmiling cat, Presto growled and showed his tiny teeth. "Who cares about training? All day long you tell me I got to stay in training. Training! What am I training for, Odacious, I'd sure like to know."

The large black cat grinned in spite of himself. The li'l feller's got a bellyful of moxie, I'll give 'em that. Then, more gently, "Here I been all my life around boxing and the gloves and the ring. The ring! That's the moment of truth, when you have to prove yourself! Are you a cat...or a rat? A fighter...or a whiner? Which are you, Presto?"

Quick as thought the kitten answered, "I'm a fighter. I can lick my weight in junk yard dogs, Odacious. I can whip bull sharks with one paw tied behind me. I can go the distance, I tell you."

Maybe the boy got his spunk from his mamma's side, marveled Odacious. "But are you stout enough to whip Big Black Jack Johnson, little cat?"

Presto glared at his larger friend. Odacious must be the biggest cat I've ever known, the kitten wondered. But he keeps talking about somebody even bigger and meaner than himself. Who in the name of Blackbeard the Pirate is Big Black Jack Johnson, puzzled Presto. But all that came out of the astonished kitten's mouth was a squeak.

"Stick close, now Presto. We can't be late for Great-Aunt Meowkin's Reunion. There'll be plenty of groceries for you to fill up on, and maybe some kitties to dance with, too." He meowed deeply and combed his whiskers.

"Well, maybe since you won't let me eat on the way," grumbled Presto, "you might tell me who this Great-Aunt Meowkin is."

Odacious squared his shoulders and said dreamily, "Great-Aunt Meowkin was mighty nice to us Galveston Cats when this island wasn't much more than a big mudslide. She came to us after the Great Storm and single-pawed, she fed us and licked our wounds and got us where we could stand on our four feet again. Great-Aunt Meowkin, she was like family to us."

"And that's why the Galveston Cats hold a reunion for her every year," asked Presto, "and break a flounder and all that?"

"You got it, little cat," replied Odacious. "Us Galveston Cats are thriving today because of Great-Aunt Meowkin's giving ways. After the Great Storm, she helped build the seawall...but say, let's make tracks for that reunion."

Presto kept pace with Odacious for a few steps and then curiosity pulled his whiskers. The kitten tugged at the big cat's glorious tail and meowed, "Say Odacious! How 'bout telling me along the way about who this Big Black Jack Johnson was?"

Odacious nodded. The little cat ought to know about his kinfolk, particularly if he's going to become the next kitten-weight champion of the world. So the big ebony cat said, "Keep up with me now, Presto, and lend both ears to the telling. Long before you was even a sparkle in your daddy cat's eyes, there was this huge black man named Big Black Jack Johnson who lived on the island. He was a dockworker down where the big steamers used to anchor, and he worked sunup to sundown loading wooden boxes of freight on them ships."

"Ahh, a human," groaned Presto.

"Not your ordinary human," yowled Odacious. "A big, black, grinning, head shaved, gold-toothed giant of a man who could eat his weight in frog legs and smash heads like hen's eggs."

"But I thought you was gonna tell me about cats, Odacious," whined Presto. "Why should I give a care about some frog-leg eating human?"

"Ain't talking about cats now, Presto," protested Odacious. "I'm talking about the greatest boxer who ever lived, and he was born right here on Galveston Island."

Odacious shook his panther head and whistled. "A shade over 6 feet, packing maybe 210 pounds in his prime, with a flashy disposition, and a ringside chatter that would romance oysters from their beds. That was Big Black Jack Johnson, and once he was the heavyweight champion of the world!"

Presto whistled. "In the whole world, Odacious? You mean from here to Port Arthur famous?"

The big cat chuckled. "Least that far, little cat. We still got a few blocks to go, Presto. Want to hear about Big Black Jack Johnson's greatest fight?"

The kitten nodded energetically and ran circles around Odacious' dignified walk. "Betcha booty, I do," purred the kitten.

Odacious stopped to lick a ruffled hair on his great chest into place and then he began in a sing-song kind of way. "Now Big Black Jack Johnson had whipped every contender who throwed a glove at 'em. Tommy Burns, Jeff Jeffries, an Oklahoma giant named Carl Morris, he knocked 'em down and they took their sweet time getting up off the canvas. Got so after he defended his title, he'd wear a beret over his shaved head and go around in public pushing a gold-headed cane or racing a yellow sports car. Then one day he met his match."

Presto interrupted with a yowling question. "He got beat up in the ring, Odacious?"

Odacious stopped to lick a great black paw and clean an ear. "Not in the ring, little cat, though later he did get whipped and lost his title to a mountain of a boxer named Jess Willard. But even then it took 26 rounds to cash 'em in. Nope. Weren't the ring where Big Black Jack Johnson dropped for the count. Was a fight with a giant blue-green crab dethroned the champ."

"He—he fought a crab, Odacious?" squeaked Presto.

"Sure did, little cat, and that crab, he roundhoused Big Black Jack Johnson 'till he didn't know up from down. See, the champ was in Cuba hustling fights and maybe romancing the senoritas when he took a notion to go deep sea fishing. He bet a Portuguese captain he could out-armwrestle 'em, winner take all. After packing his arm in ice, the cap'n, he promised Big Black Jack Johnson he'd take the champ after the big fish early the next morning."

Up ahead the roar of traffic on the boulevard alerted the kitten to danger. Presto huddled closer to his bigger friend, partly to hear the story and partly so he wouldn't get run over flatter than a flounder this close to dinner.

Odacious felt the nervousness in the kitten's whiskers and nudged him closer to his great flanks. You're safe with me, little cat, Odacious thought. "Now that Portuguese cap'n took his ship ten or twelve miles out to sea and fished all night, but they didn't get a nibble. So the heavyweight champ of the world says to that Portuguese cap'n, 'Gimme a rope and tie me some meat on the end of it. If I can't catch marlin, believe I can catch me some kind of shark and wear his teeth 'round my neck for the next fight.'"

"But you said he got whipped by a giant blue-green crab, Odacious."

"And he did, little cat, he did. Just listen. Now, no sooner did Big Black Jack Johnson drop his line overboard than he felt a tremendous tug. The champ, he braced himself against the starboard side of that ship and held on for dear life. Slowly, hand over fist, he began pulling in what he thought was a Mako shark. Big Black Jack Johnson, he pulls and tugs, and his muscles swell and tears his shirt. Directly he hollers to the Portuguese cap'n that he can see something under the boat and to get a gaff. But what Big Black Jack Johnson had a holt of was a monster crab."

Presto's breath came in little gasps. "H-how big was that monster crab, Odacious?"

"Bigger than a house, bigger than the Portuguese cap'n's ship, bigger even than two Big Black Jack Johnsons. And it had claws bigger than telephone poles that went clackity-clack-clack at the champ's head. When Big Black Jack Johnson saw that monster blue-green crab coming at him BIG TIME, snapping and clawing at his head, he dropped that line like it was a rattlesnake."

Presto thought a spell and then he asked, "What happened to the champ after that?"

"After he recovered from the rope burns on his hands, he announced his retirement from deep-sea fishing. Then he rented a whole floor of the hotel room in downtown Havana and throwed money around like confetti. But...Big Black Jack Johnson never ate no crab again, that's for certain."

Presto nodded but persisted, "Whatever happened to that monster blue-green crab, Odacious?"

The Bombay panther cat grinned, showing his long white teeth. "Some years later they caught that crab out there past the oil rigs, cleaned out the meat, and stuffed it. We walk right past Gaido's restaurant where the old crab's plastic remains hustle seafood platters."

Presto gulped and stammered, "Wh-when we get to the reunion tonight, Odacious, don't let Percey and Evelyn put no crab cakes on my plate, will ya?"

Odacious growled panther-like and promised.

117

"Here's the boulevard, little cat. Keep a keen eye out for traffic. We're making good time for Great-Aunt Meowkin's Reunion. I can't wait to hear what them cats been up to!

Chapter Fourteen:

Argyles and the Trickster

Under the San Luis Pass toll bridge that connects Galveston Island to Freeport live the elderly, the retired, and the adventurous who fish all day and battle the flesh-eating mosquitos at night in their ancient RV's and campers. Here are no brightly-colored umbrellas planted on the swarming beach, no sweating sunbathers grilling on rainbow towels. Here the Gulf lies a hundred yards from the front bumper. And here lives the oddest couple ever to stroll the wet sands: Argyles, a precocious killdeer, and The Trickster, an American Shorthair cat, orange as the harvest moon right down to his white spats.

Argyles had rescued The Trickster early one pre-dawn morning when the tides threatened to wash him out to sea. No matter that the rescue involved hoisting The Trickster tail-first in the air over the advancing waters and dropping the orange, yowling kitten in a dry clump of Pampas grass.The Trickster immediately thanked Argyles and they became fast friends, sort of the Pancho and Cisco of the entire San Luis Pass beach head.

Now they were sauntering along the shoreline, Argyles with his impatient bird's skittering and The Trickster moving with the grace—he thought—of the King of the Beasts, except when he leaped paws-first into the little tidal pools that crisscrossed the beach. From a distance they seemed a comic pair: The Trickster with his tail listing to starboard and Argyles, flighty and high-strung, nervously pecking at his wings and dancing impatiently around his taller friend. In the wet sand Argyles' trident prints clashed with The Trickster's heavy double-toed marks.

"Arrgh, Trickster," screeched Argyles. "If you don't get a move on, we're going to be late, old buddy." The alarmed killdeer peered through tiny granny glasses at his friend.

"Chill, Will," yowled The Trickster. "We got, like, a couple hours before Great-Aunt Meowkin's Reunion. Great scallops, Argyles, what's the rush? We'll get there before Percey and Evelyn have the shrimp boiled."

Argyles screamed and threw his wings into the air. "Just because you have a cat's double-toed luck doesn't mean we're just going to be magically whisked away to the reunion. Why, we're still miles from the public beaches."

But The Trickster only sniffed his moist white button of a nose in the air. Following his quivering nostrils, The Trickster paced back and forth on the empty beach until he stood staring at the soft sand beneath his paws. Then he started digging like crazy. "Dig here, Argyles. My sniffer tells me there's buried treasure on this spot!"

Using his needle beak, Argyles joined his yowling friend in a frantic dig on the beach. Soon two little mounds of sand lay heaped on the flat ground. Just as Argyles was about to say that The Trickster's nose was full of red sauce, the shorthair flipped something golden out of the shallow pit.

It was a doubloon!

Argyles grasped the shiny coin in his little black talons and read the date: *1817*. "Arrgh, Trickster! You have uncovered LaFitte's hidden treasure chests. Keep digging."

But an hour's spirited digging later, no coins had leaped from the gaping hole in the ground, and The Trickster clawed his way up to the surface and shook his burnt-orange fur. Then he leaned back on his hind legs and began a leisurely tongue bath from the furry ankles up.

"Arrgh, Trickster, there's no time for lounging around now. We have to get to Great-Aunt Meowkin's Reunion before those silly cats, Rumpy and Stumpy, get there and eat all the mackerel."

The Trickster pulled and pulled at his matted fur and tried unsuccessfully to spit a hair ball twisted 'round his teeth. Exasperated, Argyles tugged at the snakey hairs and succeeded in wrapping his beak in cat fur. Five or six heaves later, Argyles eyed his bathing friend critically.

"If you don't just come along right now, I'll give your excuses at the reunion." Argyles tapped an angry talon on the smooth sand.

But The Trickster had dozens of spit curls that

required straightening and he didn't budge. Finally, in desperation, Argyles fumed and said, "If I tell you the story about Tuko and the giant alligator, will you shake a paw?" The little killdeer marched circles around his friend's private sauna, which had by now reached the catpits.

The Trickster stopped his licking and nodded. "You know how I like, love, your stories, Argyles." Then he moistened one paw and shampooed his ears.

"Long before this island became crowded with silly tourists and billboards, the only humans who lived here were tall, bronzed Indians. They were the Karankawa, and they once walked these same shores that you and I stroll on, Trickster. According to the first European to explore Galveston Island—a Spaniard named Cabeza de Vaca, who was shipwrecked on this island—these Karankawa warriors were big men, six feet tall, with tall hunting bows that reached their sharkoil-smeared faces. And they walked these dunes year-round without a stitch of fur or feathers."

The Trickster looked up from a hairball bigger than the doubloon he had discovered. "Like, not even whiskers, Agyles? Great flying fish!"

"And that's not all, Trickster. The men were tattooed all over their bodies and they wore pieces of cane in their lower lips and through their chests. Now wouldn't that be a difficult way to eat flounder?"

Trickster had begun a serious rinsing of his crimped tail, and for a few seconds he did not answer. Then, between kitty licks, he said to his wondering friend, "Maybe they, like, stuck fish chunks on either side of the cane. Sort of like shishkabob chest snacks, huh?"

Argyles shook his head. "Arrgh, Trickster. There's no record of de Vaca seeing that among the Karankawas, and I've got Mr. J. Frank Dobie's copy right here." Argyles produced a tiny, red-covered book from inside his feathered vest pocket.

The Trickster gaped. "Where did you learn to read, Argyles?"

The little scavenger bird tweedled and danced from toe to toe. "Do you take me for a bird brain, Trickster? Great-Aunt Meowkin tutored me in my letters and provided me with the finest classics."

The Trickster grinned. "Alright already, Argyles. Like, don't get your feathers wet. See! I'm finished with my bath, ready to journey on to Great-Aunt Meowkin's Reunion."

A series of mournful hoots erupted from Argyles' beak. "I fear we'll be late again, Trickster. But if you get your glorious tail in gear, perhaps we can arrive before the halibut ice cream. Shall I continue with my story?"

Trickster nodded enthusiastically and the two friends continued their journey down the beach as the late-afternoon sun slowly dipped behind a swirl of scudding clouds.

"See, it was like this, Trickster," whispered Argyles, feeling important again now that he had the big cat's undivided attention. "Tuko was the oldest son of the chief of the Karankawas, and one afternoon, perhaps an afternoon much like this one, Trickster, Tuko overheard his mother tell his father the chief that the tribe was almost out of food. There wasn't even an oyster left in camp. Tuko knew that if the tribe was hungry, they would come to his father and demand meat. His father would not bear such disgrace, Tuko vowed. He, Tuko, eldest son of Chief Capoques of the Karankawa, would bring food to his people and honor for himself. That night, while everyone slept around the campfire, Tuko set out across the bay in his father's canoe."

Trickster pulled up suddenly to examine the oozing remains of a huge jellyfish. Gingerly he stepped on the evil-looking head of the Man-of-War, then, leaping free of the rotting mess, landed just inches from Argyles' pointed beak. Patiently the killdeer readjusted his spectacles.

Dashing around his feline companion, Argyles shook his tailfeathers and continued. "As I was saying, Trickster. Steadying his long pole in the shallow water, Tuko began the long trip across the bay. He knew of a secret oyster bed that no one, not even the best hunters, had ever seen before. Tuko told himself that he would load the dugout canoe with fat oysters and return to camp before any of the tribe had awakened. Then he would blow the conch shell and cry, 'Food.'

"Now traveling through the dark was breathtaking for the chief's son. Using the stars as his guide, Tuko slowly poled his canoe across the still waters. Once he heard a whirring sound ahead of him and saw a dark fin slice through the darkness, but Tuko kept his eyes on the black outline of the shore and told himself that the playful dolphins were his escorts."

"Once ashore, Tuko dug fat oysters big as his hands out of the muck and loaded them in his small boat. Then, the canoe perilously low in the water, he began the long journey back. His arms ached from poling, and his hands stung from the cuts he received handling the sharp shells, but he told himself that he would earn much honor from the tribe for this daring deed. His father might even honor him with a white shell necklace to impress the young girls."

Just then The Trickster saw in the distance the intense glare of the shops and hotels on Seawall Boulevard. "Hey Argyles, check it out! We're nearly there. I can almost, like, taste the flounder, can't you?"

The tiny bird permitted himself a hoot. "A taste is exactly what I was going to say, Trickster. A taste of meaty Karankawa, that is, if you're a twenty foot alligator."

The Trickster stopped in mid-prance and his bent tail almost stood at attention. His voice quavering, the wide-eyed cat asked, "A-a-a twenty foot alligator, Argyles?

"That's indeed what I just said," screeched the killdeer, pecking at an idle wing feather. "Tuko was so busy making up stories about himself that he didn't see the Vshaped ripples heading straight for his boat. Too late! The huge reptile's nasty snout clamped down on the stern of Tuko's tiny skiff, upending oysters and the boy into the bay. While the toothy monster gorged himself on shellfish, Tuko clambered onto the back of the overturned canoe and screamed for help. But he was too far from shore and his people lay sound asleep."

"Well, great barracudas, Argyles! What did Tuko do?" The Trickster's kinked tail weaved like a cobra's head at a Hindu snake ceremony.

"The alligator finished with the oysters and then he came at the boy. Slowly he began crawling his way up the bark-lined canoe, his evil red eyes glittering like hot coals in the darkness. The great beast opened and shut his terrible jaws and Tuko heard the horrid clatter of five inch teeth snapping and rending the air. When the alligator was just inches from Tuko's head, he lunged, his disgusting hot breath blasting Tuko's face, and his mouth locked squarely on...Tuko's wooden pole!"

Poor Trickster collapsed on the beach. "You mean, like, the alligator dude didn't bite off Tuko's head?"

Making scooting sounds as he walked on the frothy ebb of waves, Argyles shook his head. "Oh, that hungry alligator bit down hard as he could, but he couldn't snap in two that stout wooden pole imbedded in his mouth. Fact is, the harder that alligator struggled, the tighter the pole wedged in his mouth. Frantically, Tuko paddled with his hands and feet, desperately trying for shore before the alli-

128

gator crushed the pole with his enormous jaws. When he reached the surf, Tuko leaped off and ran straight into camp, where he seized his father's long bow and arrows. When he returned to the shore, there was that great monster alligator, floating belly-up in the surf. The greedy lizard had rolled off the canoe, pitched into two feet of water, and drowned."

Perplexed, Trickster asked, "Like, how did a twenty foot alligator drown in the surf, Argyles?"

"Simple, you cat-astrophic feline," whistled the energetic killdeer. "That big 'gator had the pole in his mouth, didn't he, and he couldn't break it, now could he? So when he fell into the waves, he swallowed once, twice, and then..." Argyles made a puffing sound like a blowfish, swelled up his feathers until he was twice his normal size, and then keeled over in the wet sand. He lay there, a stuffed bird if ever there was one. Then he stood up, adjusted his white collar, flicked a wingful of sand off his wings, and bowed deeply.

"Great Ridley Turtles, Argyles, that's an awesome story!" whooped The Trickster. "Will you, like, tell it again tonight for the Galveston Cats at Great-Aunt Meowkin's Reunion?"

The little killdeer hooted like an owl. "IF we ever get there, Trickster. Look! The sun is setting and here we are jabbering away like gossiping seagulls. Let's move some tail or we're going to miss the breaking of flounder and the Ceremony at the Seawall.

And saying that, the little killdeer scooted down the beach, leaving The Trickster to catch up with the tiny bird's trident tracks. "Like, wait up for me, Argyles!" he yowled.

Chapter Fifteen:

Rumpy and Stumpy go Fishing for Whales

Around dusk the restless tides enflame the blood of humans and cats and the Seawall sidewalk bristles with barefoot traffic. Many a night has seen hard-luck fishermen with ice coolers over their shoulders march up the ramp to the fishing piers stretching like outstretched arms into the Gulf. Tourists too, wasted after a day's steaming drive in the Texas heat, ramble by two's and three's to the bait shop where they size up the high cost of landing a fishing spot beyond the chain link fence.

Once these would-be anglers realized how much ocean-caught fish costs per ounce, they content themselves with a leisurely stroll down the ramp and a shrimp basket to go under the sign of the great white shark at Miller's Landing.

In the shadows of the 61st Street Fishing Pier huddled Rumpy and Stumpy, arguing as usual over who deserved first pick of the beachcombing treasures spilling out of a torn crabbing net. An hour's promenade down the beach had yielded the two cats an astonishing collection of shells, fish heads, gull feathers, odd-shaped pieces of driftwood, and enough seaweed to choke a white whale.

"No, you don't Stumpy." hissed Rumpy. "You know I found those abalone shells, and say, that hermit crab belongs to me. Give it back!"

"You're just hissing in the wind," yowled Stumpy. "These shells are going around the neck of the prettiest kitty I meet at Great-Aunt Meowkin's Reunion."

"Are NOT!"

"Are TOO!"

While the two Manx tubby tabbies fought tooth and claw over their swag, the hermit crabs mustered in a shallow pool and silently marched back into the surf. Too late! Stumpy looked up from his half-nelson on Rumpy's thumb-sized tail to see the last of the crabs scuttle into the foam.

"Now look what you did, Rumpy," he screeched. "You let all the crabs get away. Now what are we going to give the kitties for presents?"

Rumpy gasped for breath and wheezed, "W-Why don't we slip over to the fishing pier and try our luck catching a tarpon."

"Give me a break, Rumpy," Stumpy growled. "Nobody's caught a tarpon off one of those fishing piers since One-Eyed Tom was knee-high to a pinfish. But say," Stumpy whistled, "maybe pier fishing ain't such a bad idea." A flash of white and pink had caught the roving tom's eye, and quick as thought, he scooped up the dripping wet contents of the net and dashed to the ramp.

"Hey, wait up, Stumpy," called Rumpy. "What's the big rush?"

"That, fishbreath!" And Stumpy pointed in the direction of the flash of white and pink. "Don't you see her?"

She was beyond beautiful. Sleek, long-haired, white as cockleshells, she flounced from fisherman to fisherman, sniffing their bait buckets, offering advice where to cast the writhing hooks, and, to every tom cat from here to the Bolivar Lighthouse, she was a kitty with an attitude.

Around her wispy neck hung a silver chain and necklace which stated to anyone who bothered to read it that Miss KitKat was the property of Billy Buddy and she was three years old and had had all her shots. But what gave tomcats the howling blues was this: tied to the end of her glorious tail was a perfect pink satin ribbon. She was the cat's meow and she knew it.

Rumpy and Stumpy gawked at Miss KitKat until they melted like salted snails into the damp sand. After a while they stood up, wailing like coyotes at a full moon, and charged up the ramp where they waited for a bus group of parched tourists to poke along up the ramp. The two cats scampered through a forest of hairless legs until they reached the bait shop.

"How we gonna get past her owner," whispered Rumpy, gasping for breath.

"Easy," wheezed Stumpy. "We'll wait for him to get distracted and then we'll make a run for it. Remember, I gave you my shells in return for talking to that kitty first."

Rumpy scratched his head and started to argue, but Stumpy hushed him with one outstretched paw. An elderly man who walked and talked like he had hit every grog shop along the boulevard demanded to be served a shrimp po-boy.

"Ain't got sandwiches here, mister," fumed Billy Buddy. "This here's a bait shop. We sell bait shrimp for fishing, not eating."

But the elderly man protested so loudly that the fishermen out by the windswept piers made faces through the windows. In desperation, Billy Buddy held up two slices of white bread and slimed them with blood bait. Then he dropped a half dozen tiny pale shrimp on the dripping bread.

"Here mister, eat this. Hope you don't want no fries, 'cause all I got is squid parts."

While the raving old fool devoured the sandwich and demanded his fries, Rumpy and Stumpy hustled through the gate and found six silent fishermen casting and baiting and maybe praying for a nibble. Then they saw Miss KitKat and the world exploded in fireworks.

Her golden eyes locked with Stumpy's green ones and she hissed at him. "What are you two garbage cats doing here on my pet human's fishing pier? Scat, you bad trashbag rippers, or I'll yowl for him and he'll throw the both of you into the drink."

136

But Stumpy had Miss KitKat in his arms and had begun licking her whiskers energetically.

"Get away from me, you...you backfence Cats-anova," shrieked Miss KitKat. "NO nasty-smelling tomcat embraces me unless I give him permission." She scrambled under the legs of a half-asleep fisherman and sat there, hissing like an inflated adder at both felines.

"That's a fine way to greet the world's greatest fisher-cat," smiled Stumpy. "Why, I'm known from here to Hong Kong for my unbelievable catches."

"Hmph! You couldn't catch minnows in a bucket," sniffed Miss KitKat.

"Tell her who I am," said Stumpy.

"Uhh, that's right, Miss KitKat. This here's Queequeg Stumpy, the South Seas Cat-O-Nine-Hooks. He's caught marlin in the Caribbean, great white sharks off the coast of Australia, and...." Rumpy gasped for breath.

"And whales in the South Pacific," said Stumpy, giving Miss KitKat his best Rhett Butler smile. "Well said, Tashtego Rumpy. If I land the biggest fish this pier has ever weighed, will you go with me to Great-Aunt Meowkin's Reunion?"

Miss KitKat considered the invitation. True, he looked like a rascal, and a liar to boot, but something tinkled like wind chimes when he talked. Besides, she told herself, when the crowd thinned out, her pet human liked to turn out the lights and watch boring reruns on TV. Going to the reunion beat weighing bait shrimp, she told herself.

"Alright, Cap'n Ahab. Here's a pole and there's a spot over there," she purred. "Catch me a whale, you big cat."

Smiling like a Cheshire cat, Stumpy took the pole in his hands and nudged Rumpy, who awoke from his trance staring at Miss KitKat's pink ribbon and poked a paw into the bait bucket. Gingerly he pulled out something red and bleeding and quickly handed it to Stumpy, who held his breath and hooked the oozing lump of flesh onto his hook and made a long cast past the breakers.

"Hmmmm," purred Miss KitKat. "You do know something about fishing now, don't you?"

Holding the pole in one paw and wrapping his free paw around Miss KitKat's slim waist, Stumpy expounded on his fishing trophies won from New Cat-adonia to North Cat-olina.

"Yep, Miss KitKat, you're going out with the greatest fishercat ever to wet a line. Why, back five or six years ago me and my sidekick here, Tashtego Rumpy, charted a boat and went 'round the world in search of the great fish. Two days out of Tokyo we hooked a fifty foot humpback that towed the ship seven days and seven nights, and me holding that line from morning to night, with only one catnap and a little 2% milk."

"Oh my," nuzzled Miss KitKat, "What a big, strong, fishercat you are, Queequeg Stumpy."

Rumpy interjected with his own version. "Uh-huh. When the whale finally came up for air, we harpooned him until his backside looked like a pin cushion. Then we...."

"Ah, Tashtego, hand me some more of that invigorating bait. Anyway, my dear, when the whale breached, I leaped upon his back and plunged my silver harpoon into his neck until he spouted black blood. Then I tied rope to his tail and we towed that blubber all the way to Santa Catalina and fed the entire cat population for a month."

Just then there was a tremendous tug on the taut fishing line and Stumpy yelled, "I got a whale! I got a whale!"

The dozing fishermen awoke from their marlin fantasies and crowded around Stumpy. The Manx gritted his teeth and pulled and tugged on his line. Miss KitKat stood close by, offering advice and licking Stumpy's ears for encouragement.

Through heaving gasps, Stumpy whooped, "Tashtego Rumpy, this whale must be even larger than the great humpback we caught last summer off the coast of Alaska!"

Rumpy stood transfixed, gazing at Miss KitKat. Finally, Stumpy tipped the bait bucket on Rumpy's hind legs and the Manx hopped from one wet paw to the other.

"Uh, right, Queequeg Stumpy. Blue whales off Jessica Point, south of Seward."

Suddenly the creature hooked on Stumpy's line gave a tremendous lurch and the cat slammed into the railing. Miss KitKat screamed, "My hero!" Through smashed lips Stumpy called, "Rumpy, er, Tashtego, give me a hand NOW!"

Rumpy grabbed Stumpy around his fat tummy and pulled for all he was worth. Together the two fat cats fought the fish, and slowly, very slowly, they pulled, paw over paw, the quivering line.

"I tell you, Miss KitKat, this is the biggest whale since Jonah slapped gloves with a behemoth. Every cat on the island will have whale fritters for weeks after I land this Monstro."

Miss KitKat swooned and placed her dainty white paws around Stumpy's neck. "What a tomcat!" she purred.

But the great fish still had fight and twice more the two weary cats were slammed into the railing, leaving throbbing bumps and spinning Tweety Birds cat-calling past their slitted eyes.

Finally, after a spirited half-hour's pulling and teeth-gritting, the struggling fish tired and Stumpy began to make headway. "Any moment now, my dearest, and that whale will break the surface and I'll harpoon him with my...Tashtego, did you forget my harpoon?"

Rumpy fumbled for words. "Ah, harpoon, Stumpy? I mean, Queequeg?"

A final, heart-stopping wrenching of the pole, and the hooked creature broke water and struggled in the air. The fishermen stared over the railing at the catch and began to laugh like madmen.

"Monstro the whale, right, boys?" smirked Stumpy.

But Rumpy had peered over the railing and made snorting sounds through his wet nose. "Ahh, Queequeg, I don't think you're gonna need that silver harpoon."

Miss KitKat, leaning over Stumpy's shoulder, yelled, "Land him Tashtego, and I'll gaff the monster."

With his last ounce of strength, Stumpy whipped the beastie over the railing and down on the wet pier flopped— a four inch perch!

Miss KitKat stared at the twitching fish and looked from Stumpy to Rumpy, who stood there grinning like village idiots.

"Well," began Stumpy, "it sure FELT like a whale."

"Fought like one too," echoed Rumpy.

Miss KitKat saw red. "Get out of here NOW, you lying deadbeats. A whale! That perch isn't big enough to fillet, you scoundrels." She began to throw anything she could get her paws on at the embarrassed felines.

"Ow," hollered Stumpy, as the bait bucket bounced off his head. "Don't! Please don't, Miss KitKat."

"Get off my fishing pier NOW, you bloated toads," hissed Miss KitKat, "or I'll use this fishing pole for a cat-o-nine-tails on the both of you."

Both tomcats dashed down the ramp, and when they were a safe distance from Miss KitKat's rage, Stumpy called out, "Does this mean you're breaking our date to Great-Aunt Meowkin's Reunion?"

A tempest of dead fish rained on Rumpy and Stumpy. Even from a distance the two frightened cats could hear Miss KitKat calling them cat-aclysmic names.

"Guess she ain't gonna go with you to the reunion," kidded Rumpy, pulling a stinking mudcat off his head.

"Shut up and help me fill this net with fish," growled Stumpy. "Leastways we got appetizers for the evening feast."

Slowly the two tomcats hiked up the beach as the sun yawned purple and began to slip out of sight. In a few minutes Stumpy began to whistle.

"What are you whistling for, Stumpy? Ain't you upset Miss KitKat called you a catty-wampus ?"

"Ahh, who wants to go out with a kitty who wears a pink ribbon on her glorious tail, anyway? There's plenty more fish in the seas, Rumpy."

Rumpy began to laugh and he couldn't stop. Finally, after much coaxing by Stumpy, he gasped for air and said, "Well, in your case, Queequeg, it ain't just fish. It's perch."

Stumpy started to hit Rumpy up the side of the head and then caught himself. "Hey, it WAS a whale of a tale, after all. Maybe we'll tell it again at Great-Aunt Meowkin's Reunion tonight."

Chapter Sixteen:

Trips Battles the Cat-Eating Clam

An hour before sunset, as the breeze off the ocean refreshed weary fishermen and buoyed the spirits of sunburned tourists, a late model station wagon lurched up to the curb on Seawall Boulevard and a middle-aged couple hopped out and stood facing the incoming tide. For a long time neither spoke, then cautiously, the bespectacled man looked up and down the busy sidewalk. Then he nodded to his female companion and from deep pockets they pulled packets of dry cat food.

Where the tumble of rough hewn granite blocks divided the brown beach from the concrete seawall, a small ledge formed and here the retired cat lovers filled aluminum pie pans with food. They watched as from under clefts in the great stones abandoned cats of all sizes, shapes, and colors crept up on the feeding ledge and crunched the star-shaped cat food. These lank and lean felines were the Galveston Cats and over the years the toms and cattas had raised proud litters that now helped themselves to bitesized morsels of chicken and veal cereal.

While the couple fussed over the Galveston Cats like the furballs were their own children, one cat, a strongly-built Maine Coon, twirled his glorious raccoon tail and watched the parade of tourists and islanders parade down the sidewalk. This city never sleeps, Trips told himself.

There'll be this much traffic at three in the morning, compulsive joggers and insomniacs running like grunion to the rhythm of the tides. Trips yowled, his great lynx-like face all teeth and tongue, while the old couple congratulated themselves for saving the Galveston Cats another day.

Suddenly two bully American Wirehairs, their prickly hair matted and twisted like grunge cats, shoved a tiny kitten off an aluminum plate where she was feeding, and planted their dirty paws in the food. Between crunchy bites, they laughed at the crying kitten who mewed piteously as she clung by one paw to the edge of the boulder. Trips growled deep in his throat, a wild snarl, part lynx and part bobcat, and the two Wirehairs glared at the Maine Coon's electric fur. Swiftly, Trips grabbed each cat's skull in a huge paw, smashed them together like coconuts, and grinned as the two dazed felines oozed down the rocks and collapsed on the wet sand below.

The old couple on the beach applauded the great cat's prowess, and Trips bowed to them. The Rosenkatz are good humans, Trips thought, and they'd make good pets for some cast-off Galveston Cat who needs regular helpings of canned milk and a warm fire to curl up beside. The kitten's frantic mewing shattered Trips' daydream, and he looked down to see the little one holding on by two tootsies.

"Ayah! Keep your fur dry, princess, Trips will save you," said the beefy cat, lowering his glorious tail for the squealing kitten to climb up on. Once she had gripped Trips' thick mane of striped tail, the Maine Coon lowered the kitten on the boulder where he sat. Poor little thing,

Trips thought, gazing at the shivering kitten, she needs a home BIG TIME. He looked back at the sidewalk where the Rosenkatz had stood admiring Trips' handiwork on the Wirehairs, but they were two blocks down Seawall Boulevard.

"Ayah! Shame you didn't purr for the Rosenkatz, princess. They might have taken you in. Imagine! Whole saucers of cream every morning. Don't take my word for it, kitten, but that kind of room service beats daybreak on these cold boulders all hollow. Say, princess, got a name?" Trips nudged the kitten under the chin while the remaining Galveston Cats munched away.

"My momma called me Abigail," said the tiny kitten, "NOT princess. When her pet human became angry with her for having my brothers and sisters, he just dropped us here in a cardboard box and roared off in his car. Last week two mean boys were throwing rocks at us...and... one of the rocks hit my momma and...." The kitten began wailing. Trips looked around nervously and smiled weakly as one or two of the Galveston Cats stared hard at the sobbing kitten.

"Ayah, hush up there, Abigail. Here, compose yourself with this kitty treat." Trips offered the teary-eyed kitten a half-eaten stick of beef jerky. "Go ahead, be my guest. I got lots of them down in my bunk."

By degree Abigail stopped snuffling, and Trips even allowed her to dry her black button of a nose on his glorious tail. Just another Household Pet shipwrecked on these rocks, Trips told himself, watching the kitten playing with her tail. She's a little cutie, all white and black and orange calico, and she'd make some little Rosenkatz happy to cuddle her.

"Be dark right soon now, Abigail. Fancy going to a real feast with me and some of the local heroes here? Tonight's Great-Aunt Meowkin's reunion, and we always break a flounder in her memory and share in the Ceremony. Be lots of fish and kitties there, I reckon."

Abigail nodded vigorously. "I've never been off these rocks, Mister Trips, and I'd be scared if you didn't protect me from the mean humans. My momma, she told me, never rub up against mean boys wearing bandanas. My momma...." and the kitten began boo-hooing again, which is prolonged cat screeching indeed.

"Here now, no more tears. You just stick with Trips, and he'll take care of you. I've lived on this island seven years and three cat lives, and I know every sand dune and low tide ripple like the back of my paw." The large black and yellow-banded Maine Coon helped his little friend off the boulders and onto the beach. Pointing a great paw down the beach, Trips said, "See that glow in the distance? That's the driftwood bonfire where the reunion's going on as we speak. Wait 'till you meet some of the cats on this island."

"Who is this Great-Aunt Meowkin, Mister Trips?" asked Abigail.

The Galveston Cats up on the boulders heard

Abigail's question and began to yowl. "SHE DON'T KNOW WHO GREAT-AUNT MEOWKIN IS?" Trips roared, a very easy thing for a cat half-lynx and half-bobcat to do, and said, "Great-Aunt Meowkin is practically the great-grandmother of the Galveston Cats, Abigail. See, there was this incredible storm, many years ago, that nearly washed the island into the sea. Thousands of cats and humans drowned when the Great Storm struck here on this very night. Great-Aunt Meowkin was one of the lucky survivors, and she swore that she would give her nine lives to rejuvenating the cat population and rebuilding the ruined city."

"So Great-Aunt Meowkin is really the Mother Cat of us all, Mister Trips?" asked the astonished kitten. Behind her in packs of two's and three's the Galveston Cats began to make their way off the boulders and close up ranks behind Trips and Abigail.

"Ayah! Now I don't know about that. My daddy was pure Down East lynx from Caribou, Maine. But I was raised up islander, Abigail, as were all my friends," waving his great fuzzy arms to embrace the furry tide of Galveston Cats behind them. "Let's shake tail, you cats, or we're gonna miss Percey and Evelyn's smorgasbord of paw snacks."

"Will you tell me a story along the way, Mister Trips? Storytelling makes the time go faster," minced the little calico.

"Ayah! Think I'll tell about the time I squared off

with the giant cat-eating clam of the Cocos Islands. Sailin'
with Cap'n Dewey, ex-Navy down to his bell bottom blues,
he was, with a backbone hard and straight as the mainmast.
Didn't smile much, but his sapphire eyes could twinkle
when he laughed at his own jokes, and...."

"What about the giant cat-eating clam, Mister
Trips?" persisted Abigail.

"Sure you don't have some terrier in you, Abigail?
Just won't leggo the bone, so to speak. Ayah! Anyway, me
and Cap'n Dewey was running off the Coral Sea Reefs, and
we decide to anchor in a quiet lagoon and dive for clams.
Not eating clams, kitty, pearl clams. Pearls big as pie pans,
pearls the color of cream that you can see your whiskers in,
pearls that fetch the big money. Get my drift, Abigail?"

Behind the kitten stretched a growing line of purring
and yowling felines, nose to tail, all highstepping Galveston
Cats marching down the beach.

"So we dives, Cap'n Dewey and me, and there she
blowed! Five fathoms deep in crystal blue waters, the
biggest clam I'd ever seen, and locked up tighter than the
vaults of Fort Knox. Cap'n Dewey tried to wrench the clam
apart, but he only bruised his knuckles. Question was, how
were we going to get that giant clam to open up so's we
could plunder the pearl.

"Then I had an underwater inspiration, Abigail.
Cap'n Dewey loved spicy food; he was always cooking up
a pot of beans or chili, and I made paw signals that I was

going to swim back to the boat and raid the pantry. Cap'n Dewey, he gives me a 'thumbs up' and I catpaddle back to our ship and find in the cupboard a full bottle of habenero sauce. Ammunition for that clam, don't you see, and I dive back into the water. What I didn't count on was the huge grey dorsal fin slowly gliding into the lagoon."

A chorus of meows rose in the throats of the Galveston Cats. "HAMMERHEAD!"

"Have any of your friends heard this story before, Mister Trips?" politely asked Abigail.

"Ayah, maybe one or two," Trips apologized. "So I dived down to where that stubborn clam lay on the lagoon floor, and Cap'n Dewey, he laughs bubbles when I showed him that bottle of habenero. Together we pried a crack in that shell-back's opening and drained the bottle. Then we waited. In about two shakes of a lobster tail the clam hiccuped a flurry of bubbles. He bumped and lurched like a possessed clothes dryer on the sandy lagoon bottom, and then he up and heaved a white pearl big as a beach ball into Cap'n Dewey's astonished hands. Ayah! That was one smoked clam."

"What about the hammerhead, Mister Trips?" asked Abigail.

"Funny thing about sharks. They'll circle and circle, every time prowling closer and closer before they make a lunge at you that's nothing but teeth and dead eyes. When that T-headed varmint made for us, I lured it straight for the giant clam that was still belching clouds of steam. Soon as it swam through the gasping shell, that clam slammed shut and..."

A yowling of high-pitched wails scattered the scavenger seagulls to flight. "AND THE HAMMERHEAD GOT SHUT DOWN!"

Embarrassed, Trips nodded. His paws made like an open clam's maw that slowly closed and from somewhere came a squeaky voice, "Oh no, Mister Bill!" Abigail stared at the great paws and then she fell on her back and rolled in the damp sand, giggling as only a catnipped kitten can. "That's the neatest story, Mister Trips."

"Ayah! And later that night Cap'n Dewey and I toasted each other a tall glass of buttermilk and took turns staring at our reflection in that huge shiny white pearl."

Up ahead the Galveston Cats could hear the sound of merrymaking, a great caterwauling of aroused felines dancing and singing around a flickering bonfire that grew larger and hotter as the tribe of cats came closer.

"Reunion's already started, Abigail. I promise you an evening you won't soon forget, kitty." And with those words, Trips scooped up the amazed calico and set her on his great furry head.

"Just hold on to my ears, but not too tightly, Abigail," said Trips. Looking past his glorious tail, the kitten saw the Galveston Cats pressing closer for a look. "All right, you stripes and solids and calico wonders," yowled Trips, "time for some cattin' 'round!"

The Galveston Cats streamed around Trips, making tracks for the driftwood bonfire and the trays of paw snacks Percey and Evelyn had carefully arranged. Eveyln looked up from nibbling a kipper and saw the hungry cats bearing down on him.

"There goes the neighborhood," he remarked to Percey, who was helping himself to a second slice of snapper.

"Oh, stop being catty, Evelyn," growled Percey. "Great-Aunt Meowkin loved a party herself. Goodness knows, most of the guest list are her own relations."

Overhead the new moon, a circle of darkness in an infinite sea of crystal points, began slowly to glow and whisker by whisker the MoonCat's face materialized into view. For this was indeed the night of Great-Aunt Meowkin's Reunion.

Chapter Seventeen:
Great-Aunt Meowkin's Reunion Night

The great driftwood fire crackled and threw glowing cinders high into the soft night air as the Galveston Cats danced and skipped around the flames. The stars came out and the waves rippled with pinpoints of celestial light. The gentle lapping of the surf invited the bolder cats to leap like jackfish in the frothy waters and then scamper back to the warmth of the blazing fire where they wrung out their glorious tails on the damp sands.

Ninja Jules and Miss Panders in tow with cranky Chester had arrived at the place where Great-Aunt Meowkin had gone to the Other Shore, and they had collected pawfuls of driftwood washed ashore for the reunion's bonfire. Even Chester at one point went from supervising to collecting and tugged ashore an enormous section of sun-dried palm, too big for burning, as a wooden bench for the cats to sit on and yowl their songs.

Percey and Evelyn had, as usual, arrived somewhat late but made their apologies and busied themselves with setting out paper plates of fresh kippers and sliced fillets of snapper. At one point the two pudgy cats ran off in different directions to get paw snacks and slammed into each other, scattering fish morsels everywhere.

"Are you old cats practicing for a slam dancing contest?" snickered Miss Panders. Percey was about to growl something about long-haired Persians and their work ethic, but Evelyn silenced him by slamming a cold perch on his plate. Grumbling, Percey continued heaping anchovies on the trays.

Up from San Luis Pass padded The Trickster and Argyles, toting pickle buckets of yummy clams pecked out of the soft mud by the sharp-eyed killdeer. The Trickster wowed everyone with his pirate doubloon and polished it with Evelyn's glorious tail. Then, while Evelyn was stoking the smoldering driftwood with a herring bone, he tied oyster shells to Evelyn's glorious tail and for twenty minutes the poor old dear thought the beach was haunted. Finally, Argyles let Evelyn in on the joke and the elderly Chartreux screeched chastisements in Latin and chased The Trickster into the surf with a piece of burning driftwood.

From downtown waltzed in Odacious and Presto with a grocery sack crammed with jars of red sauce, hot relish, and catnip treats. Ninja Jules was amazed to see the two black cats retrieve sack after sack of barbequed scallops that the old sparring partner for Smokey Joe Felix had grilled the morning of the feast.

A sudden tooting of a car horn announced the arrival of Tabitha and Pyewackit who unloaded tote bags full of po-boy rolls and sliced veggies cut into mudpuppy shapes. Pyewackit used her glorious tail as a duster on a portable plastic table and Tabitha heaped the tasty goodies an armfull at a time until Presto observed that the table's legs looked like a wobbly sailor's. Even Chester, rubbing his throbbing leg in the shadows of the great fire, cackled at that one.

And then One-Eyed Tom appeared out of nowhere, hauling a huge fisherman's net of oysters he had uncovered in a secret bed that only he, raising his voice above the tumult of yowls and meows, could locate. He waved to Chester and offered him a tasty plump morsel to suck down, and Chester, grinning like Sylvester swallowing Tweety, gratefully accepted the edible gift from the old crabber. Then they began a spirited conversation about the best place to hunt tiger sharks and for all the sushi in Singapore they sounded like two retired admirals in their catnip cups.

To no one's surprise, Rumpy and Stumpy material-ized empty-handed and immediately began accusing each other of nibbling the kitty bits. When the chorus of howls drowned their pathetic voices, The Trickster crept up behind the two tomcats and grabbed their beachcombing net of treasures.A real catfight might have exploded in fur balls and teeth had not Tabitha intervened and made The Trickster return the beach toys in return for Rumpy and Stumpy's promise to play janitor after the reunion ended. Reluctantly the two Manx agreed, and then Stumpy made eye contact with Pyewackit and, nudging his brother, made for the kitten like she was caviar.

"Yuk!" Pyewackit groaned. "You two smell like blood bait! Get away from me or I'll tell Tabitha, and she'll turn you both into barnacles."

157

The threat worked. Rumpy and Stumpy took turns waiting on Pyewackit and Miss Panders, who immensely enjoyed the royal treatment. "Come next year's reunion, some nice tomcat may do that for you, Pyewackit." The Persian kitten pouted, but she knew that her human pet was right. You can't dance with a tom, Tabitha had reminded the kitten, until you can feel the music.

Then, just as Chester tossed another chunk of fire-wood on the blaze, illuminating the beach head with the dancing shadows of the Galveston Cats, Trips staggered in, blowing like a nor'easter. Riding shotgun on the Maine Cat's head sat Abigail, holding the great cat's ears like tiny reins. The kitten meowed vigorously, "Help me down, Mister Trips, so I can eat some fish."

Trips tenderly placed the excited kitten on the wet sand and stood with furry legs crossed while he caught his breath. "Ayah! Think you gained some weight since dinner there, Abigail," he groaned. Then he beckoned to the kitten with an enormous paw.

"Two plump long-hairs over there helping them-selves to the kippers are Percey and Evelyn. They were Great-Aunt Meowkin's attendants and every year they serve as the reunion's hosts. They're harmless unless you get in their way in the serving line." Trips laughed and pointed again.

"Little bird over there skittering in the surf is Argyles, the smartest killdeer on the whole island. Has a buddy named The Trickster, who's about a dozen shrimp shy of a full pound, if you ask me. Oh, and that pair of cats welded together at the whiskers is Ninja Jules and Miss Panders."

Trips looked around the bonfire, waving at the Galveston Cats helping themselves to the paw snacks. "Almost wish the Rosenkatz were here to share in the fun," he yowled, "but they turn in early."

As the cats rejoiced and leaped and feasted on the good things to eat, voices on the water could be faintly heard and then more distinctly. To everyone's amazement, two surfer cats in wet suits landed on the shore and beached their boards.

"Be this party open for Rasta cats, man?" yelled Nubs.

"Yah, man, we surf from other side of island to party down wid yo Galveston Cats," echoed Nibs.

One-Eyed Tom hugged both surfer cats and introduced his new friends to the assembly of cats. "These here surfer dudes are me shipmates, ya cats, and I hope that youse will welcome 'em aboard."

Taking the hint, Evelyn and Percey slunk up to Nibs and Nubs and offered them paper plates filled with cod tails and spicy escargot. The Jamaican surfer cats gratefully accepted the tasty party favors and even contributed four flying fish that had landed on their waxed boards.

"We eat dem raw in Jamaica," hollered Nubs. "But yo can just throw dem on de coals 'till der tails be crispy."

Odacious and Presto waved their glorious tails in the bonfire's light and the four black cats immediately began a lively conversation on the possibilities of surfing to Jamaica. Trips predicted such a voyage would require the mother of all waves, and Nibs and Nubs agreed.

When the bonfire began to die down, Chester limped into the glooming darkness and began picking up more wood. He had just unearthed a long section of smooth oak when he saw a pair of golden eyes staring up at him.

"Come into the light, blast ye, or I'll make shrimp hash outta ye with this here driftwood," growled Chester. Some mongrel dog abandoned by flaky tourists, the old shark-fighter said to himself.

But no. What emerged from the darkness was a very beautiful white kitty wearing a long strand of pink ribbon on the tip of her glorious tail.

"I-I-I don't mean to intrude, sir, I was only looking for two stump-tailed tom cats who go by the names of Queequeg Stumpy and Tashtego Rumpy. They invited me to something called Great-Aunt Meowkin's Reunion tonight. Is this it?" Miss KitKat trembled in the night air.

"Ain't no tomcat here with that name, missy. Now just you head back down that beach where you came from. They ain't no handouts for the uninvited," grumbled Chester, pushing at the terrified kitty's shoulders.

"Hold on a second," shouted Argyles. The little

killdeer dashed up to the milky white kitty, inspected her closely through his granny glasses, and tapped his feet on the beach.

"Arrgh! Only two cats who would use such ridiculous aliases," Argyles observed. "Hey, Rumpy, Stumpy. Do either of you know this young thing here?"

The two tomcats hustled over to where Miss KitKat stood shivering in the darkness. Stumpy saw the kitty and yowled like crazy.

"I knew you would come, Miss KitKat. Here, let me escort you to the fire. Tashtego Rumpy, take her belongings and set them by the fire."

As Stumpy led Miss KitKat into the fierce light of the bonfire, Rumpy picked up two large buckets brimming with trout. "Ugh, these are heavy," he groaned.

"I hope you didn't mind my coming," purred Miss KitKat. "My pet human said I could go, long's as I didn't meet up with any garbage cats. And I did bring some refreshments," pointing to the buckets Rumpy dragged in the sand, "for the reunion."

"Let me escort m'lady to a choice seat by the fire where she may warm herself and comfort her glorious tail," Stumpy said grandly, extending his bent arm for Miss KitKat to intertwine with his own.

"What a gentlecat," marveled Miss KitKat, mincing to a seat on Chester's smooth bench by the bonfire.

"Attention, all you cats, attention," called Tabitha over the merrymaking. "Now that everyone seems to be partying down, I thought we might take a moment to remember, darlings, why we're here tonight."

All the cats became quiet and a hush unbroken except for the popping of exploding cinders stilled the beach. The Galveston Cats found a stretch spot on the beach or on a piece of driftwood to hear Tabitha speak.

"On this day many years ago, Great-Aunt Meowkin went to the Other Shore. But before she died, she asked us to remember her on this same day when the Great Storm overwhelmed humans and cats alike by breaking flounder together."

The cats began caterwauling, but Tabitha silenced them with a firm wave of her hand.

"I'm sure every cat has had some portion of the goodies that we shared tonight. I know I've enjoyed my share—MEOW! But now we should entreat the moment and visualize Great-Aunt Meowkin and the Ceremony. May I ask each of you to gaze up at the moon and visualize with me?"

All the Galveston Cats stared up into the canopy of stars and one by one, they saw a wonderous thing. The shimmering face of the MoonCat beamed down at them and filled the entire beach head with a magical, silvery light. Not a cat dared to breathe or twitch a glorious tail at this supreme moment. Then a strong wind from beyond the dark sea breathed new life into the bonfire and the flames seemed to kiss the stars.

The onshore wind rippled the long, flowing red hair of Tabitha, who sat on the rocks overlooking the host of cats ringed like furry stones around the blaze.

"Visualize, darlings. Look deep into the ruby-red eyes of the MoonCat. Listen to the winds and the rhythm of the restless tides. Listen, watch, and remember!"

The Galveston Cats watched as the MoonCat grinned and seemed to snap its paws and then the wind increased in strength and the tide crashed heavily on the beach. Counter-clockwise ran the years, soaring like a great blue heron into the past, faster and faster, time all liquid now and surging like a wave until it slowed to a trickle and ebbed into shallow pools. From one of the shallow pools emerged a dripping wet kitten who shook herself off and scampered down a ruined beach. Then two small human feet stepped into the shallow pool and where the MoonCat's face had appeared on the enchanted moon now materialized a young girl's bruised features. Tears streamed down her swollen cheeks as the night air reverberated with an unearthly, high-pitched scream.

And then a hushed silence blanketed the beach and a beautiful, lyrical voice spoke from the heavens.

Chapter Eighteen:

Sacred Ceremony in the Sand

"Thank you for coming again, Galveston Cats, to Great-Aunt Meowkin's Reunion. Yes, I am that same little girl who once saved a half-drowned kitten. I am Winnie, true friend of Great-Aunt Meowkin, and there is one among you tonight who knows and loves you all."

Pyewackit made low whistling sounds and snuggled deeper in Tabitha's lap. The blushing redhead only shook her head and laughed. Below on the sand Miss KitKat dug a kitty paw into Stumpy's fat tummy.

"Is she talking about that pet human up on the rocks cuddling the little white Persian? Is she any relation to Great-Aunt Meowkin's true friend Winnie? Miss KitKat's blue eyes radiated innocence.

Stumpy nodded. "Tabitha is Winnie's only grandchild, and she's an orphan girl herself. When Winnie became too old to have children, she was led to Tabitha, who was only a kitten, so to speak, and she raised her like her own daughter. But I heard, Miss KitKat, from those plump bachelor toms, Percey and Evelyn, that Winnie taught Tabitha that visualization thing."

The soft voice continued over the waves. "After the

Great Storm, I vowed that never again would the city and its people perish. I helped raise money for a great seawall to be built that would hold back the deadly waves, and when it came time to help build that great seawall, I was there, wet and barefoot and tired—just as I was that day long ago when I clambered up from the ruins of my world!—helping to erect that barrier against the sea. Look behind you, you cats, and gaze at the great seawall that together we built!"

An ear-splitting chorus of yowls and electric whiskers erupted along the beach, scattering a tribe of marauding sand crabs. Miss Kitkat blinked up at Stumpy and, tickling his pink nose with her glorious tail, demanded an answer to her question: "The great sea wall was built by humans and cats?"

Before Stumpy could respond, the winsome voice spoke once more. "Now, you cats. Soak your paws in the surf and find the shell that calls your name!" And with that, Winnie beamed down into the calm waters and the silvery moonlight made the damp sand glitter with clam and oyster shells.

All of the Galveston Cats dashed straight for the frothy ripples where the fattest shells lay. Ninja Jules took pity on poor old gimpy Chester and tossed the limping feline a huge two-paws shell. Chester caught the shell with one furry mitt and grinned from the beach. The Trickster leaped into the waves and then howled in pain as a trickster crab pinched one claw. Argyles made sucking sounds in the surf with his muddy talons while One-Eyed Tom made a beeline for Tabitha and Pyewackit and, bowing slightly, handed a choice crustacean to Tabitha, who thanked the old crabber and stroked his furry brow. Nibs and Nubs smiled and winked at each other and tossed sand dollars on the beach next to their soaked shells.

Percey and Evelyn nibbled on lemon shark candies and sighed at one another as if to say, "Some CATS just never get out in public, poor dears."

When all of the Galveston Cats had found their shells, the voice of the woman who helped save an island continued. "Scoop out a pawful of damp sand, you cats, and shape it like a candle. And then visualize, darlings!"

Pyewackit smiled up at Tabitha, who sat with arms outstretched to the heavens, eyes closed as though in prayer. Pyewackit scooped a bit of sand with her glorious tail and sifted it into their shells. "What happens now, Tabitha?" But Tabitha was traveling in the dreamtime and softly gestured with one hand into the sky.

A silvery something, all flaky and delicate, began to shower down on the Galveston Cats. It was that rarest of powdery magic, it was MOONDUST! Like slivers of finest crystal, lunar fallout at its most gorgeous, the moondust like shimmering white mist drifted onto the Galveston Cats and their shells. Before their amazed eyes the moondust gave shape to the damp sand, hardened and firmed it, and in a cat's-whisker, a fine candle graced the bottom of the shell.

"It's magic, Mister Trips," whispered Abigail to her

tall, rugged friend. Odacious and Presto nodded agreement while Miss Panders purred her delight. "This is just so special," she sighed.

Between one cat yowl and the next the moon shape-shifted and where the beautiful face of Winnie had beamed down on the awestruck cats, now a feline form, a dignified calico with orange and black ears and a white face, materialized. It was Great-Aunt Meowkin herself glowing up in the night sky!

As the last astral grains fell on furry shoulders, the deep purring voice spoke. "Thank you, Galveston Cats, for gathering together to break a flounder on this magical night. Long before you cats were even a chin whisker in your daddy's eyes, the Galveston Cats helped build the great seawall that holds our island together. Winnie, with her brave words and strong actions, helped convince the humans to raise the money and build the great seawall. We cats helped too! At night, while the exhausted men slept, the Galveston Cats crept up to the embankments and with our glorious tails we scooped up dirt and sand and mixed it with water and slapped it on the thick walls. We didn't want another Great Storm ravaging our island ever again! So every night we worked and did our part to save what we most cherished. And now, gaze at your candles, you cats, and see such wonderous light!"

Quicker than thought the wick ends of the candles began to glow and flicker and then burn with an intense flame. The candles caught fire from the flashing golden eyes of Great-Aunt Meowkin! A hundred paws quivered in the profound light and glorious tails frizzed electric. The moment of the Ceremony had begun.

Tabitha spoke, her voice rising above the slapping of the waves on the sandy shore. "I burn this candle in the memory of the nine orphan children who drowned as they tried to reach shelter from the storm." And Pyewackit responded, "And I burn this candle for the brave nun who tied her children to her waist with a rope and died trying to save them." One-Eyed Tom raised his candle and remembered the tough doughboys who had perished when Fort Crockett fell into the pounding surf. A litany of voices then yowled the names of fallen heroes, both human and feline, who had perished in the country's worst natural disaster. And when the great caterwauling had subsided, Tabitha gave instructions.

"Take your candle, you cats, and toss it into the great seawall. Complete the Ceremony urged upon us by Winnie and Great-Aunt Meowkin. And see! Where your candle hits the wall, it becomes sand and reminds us how we came together with one heart to save our lives and our children's lives and our island home. Together, cat and human, we have survived storm and sea and tidal wave. And we shall endure!"

All the Galveston Cats gave a mighty roar that would have done justice on the plains of Africa, and even Pyewackit clapped white paws. "That was just way cool, Tabitha," gasped Pyewackit.

Tabitha smiled and nuzzled noses. "My, haven't we

been listening to alternative radio stations, little missy." And Pyewackit just grinned and nibbled her pet human's fingers.

As though on cue, Percey and Evelyn mingled among the yowling cats and distributed the four small flounders blessed by Tabitha that morning. Each Galveston Cat took a kitty bite out of the fish and passed it to the next feline in the great furry circle. "The flounder's good," exulted Chester, "and the company's better." Miss Panders, standing next to the old sea traveler, flicked her glorious tail under Chester's chin and even Ninja Jules had to laugh at the old cat's astonished face.

Tabitha sat on the rocks above the dancing and singing Galveston Cats, thrilling to the soft wind ruffling her skirt and teasing her long red hair. Every time I come to Great-Aunt Meowkin's Reunion, she said to herself, I feel so absolutely glorious to be alive.

Her reveries were interrupted by a light huffing sound on the jumble of rocks at her feet and she looked down to see One-Eyed Tom grinning up at her. The old crabber's one good eye gleamed like Long John Silver's rubies.

"I'll tell you one thing," One-Eyed Tom said to Tabitha. "I don't know how you do that visualizing thing your grandmother taught you, but there's not a Galveston Cat who wouldn't give one of his nine lives to know how you do that trick." And the old crab cat grinned like the MoonCat. How very strange, thought Tabitha.

Tabitha smiled and, taking One-Eyed Tom's paw into hers, danced the old crabber around the blazing fire. And all night and into the wee hours the Galveston Cats sang and caroused and feasted and—yes!—remembered why they had come this way.

The End

Epilogue

The driftwood fire now lies a heap of scattered ashes and slumbering coals. The Galveston Cats have found their way back to the cool granite stones and concrete ledges for catnaps and perhaps the chance to dream on about Great-Aunt Meowkin's Reunion.

The empty beach is littered with paw marks and bird tracks, proof that a great caterwauling has rocked the beach where so many years ago a half-drowned kitten and a tough little orphan girl swore friendship.

Parked near a huge palm log sits a dented green Volvo and in the front seat sleeps a small, white Persian kitten, its glorious tail swept over her eyes. A beautiful woman, leaning against the car, weaves a long red strand of hair from her eyes. Daintily she walks barefoot across the wet sand to the shoreline where the foaming surge of tides baptizes her naked feet.

Throwing her arms wide, she inhales deeply the early morning salt air, and impulsively, unfastens her enormous bonnet and waves it high over her head. As the dawn scatters the wispy clouds, she seems transfixed on the shore, as though giving thanks for the new day.

Then, her ritual complete, she walks through the

surf, feeling the good mud squishing between her toes and leaving curious little tracks in the sand. With a sudden leap she bounds to the rock jetty and tiptoes across the great drenched stones to the place that calls in her heart. There she sits crosslegged and, arms folded, stares intently at the horizon where sky and sea embrace.

Her reverie is broken by the pitiful mewings of the sleepy white kitten who, awakened by the gulls' raucous cries overhead, leaps out of the open car window and slinks across the beach to her tall, red-haired friend. The woman on the jetty smiles and waves to the little Persian to come and sit by her. The new light of day reveals for the first time the bumper sticker on the ancient rear bumper: MAGIC HAPPENS.

And so begins a new day on the island where cats and humans feel the rhythm of the tides surging in their blood and sense the connectedness of sand and sea in their hearts. And for the woman and her kitten, gazing out to sea, the promise of life begins with the visualization of the moment. THIS MOMENT.